Dea

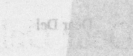

Dear Del

Alison Prince

**Hodder
Children's
Books**

a division of Hodder Headline

One

Dear Del,
You only went home this morning, but I
promised I'd write.

Why can't I think of what to say? Stare out of the window, nibble the pen. The sea's all sparkly out there, like it was when we found the hermit crabs.

A week ago, we hadn't even met.

A week ago, I was a different person.

Mum started it, of course. She's like that, always organising things and having ideas. One tea-time back in the winter, she passed the *Broray Banner* across the table to Dad, pointing at something for him to read. "We could, couldn't we?" she said, with her eyebrows up in that bright way she has.

Dad read it and shook his head. "Sounds like

1

a load of trouble to me," he said.

Barney started to laugh and bang his knife and fork on the table because he knew there was a plan being discussed, and it might be exciting. Things get a bit untidy when he does that, because he's big for fifteen, even though he's young in his mind.

Some of the experts say Barney's autistic, but Dad doesn't think so, and neither does Mum. They think he just got stuck somewhere and stopped developing. He was all right, when he was small – not that I remember, being younger.

Mum put a lump of potato back on his plate and said, "Just eat up, Barney." She retrieved the paper and passed it to me, and she and Dad looked at each other in silent argument while I read the advert she'd spotted.

> *Children's Holiday Scheme*
> *Host families wanted! Can you give a week's holiday to a boy or girl from one of Glasgow's most deprived areas? This is the only chance many of them will ever have to get a break . . .*

There was a lot more about expenses being met and how all that was needed was a willing heart and some hard work. I didn't think it sounded like hard work at all. You don't have to work at having a good time, do you? (I know now that this was a pretty naive thing to think, but at the time it sounded like a piece of cake.)

"It would be company for Fran," Mum was saying to Dad, trying to persuade him that her idea was brilliant. You'd think she might have sorted it out with him before she dragged me into it, but she's not like that. Mum's always convinced that her ideas are perfectly sensible, but it often takes a combined assault from her and me before Dad will agree. Not that he's mean or anything, but he likes time to think things over. And right now, he was not keen on being a host family to some kid from one of the grimmer parts of Glasgow.

"How do we know what we'd get?" he was saying. "It's all very well, nice idea, but having some moody adolescent from Drumchapel or somewhere in the house for a week might be no fun at all. For all you know, you might end up with a glue-sniffing shoplifter who'd be a total nightmare."

"Oh, come on, Jim," Mum said. "Talk about prejudiced! You can't write people off like that. I'm sure the Holiday Scheme people wouldn't land us with a criminal – and like I said, it would be great for Fran if we had a girl about her age.

3

You'd like that, Fran, wouldn't you?"

I nodded enthusiastically and said, "Brilliant." And I meant it. We'd been on the Isle of Broray for over a year now, and the other kids at the High School still treated me as if I came from another planet. I know I must sound a bit funny to them, having an English accent, but you'd think they'd be used to it by now, seeing there's quite a lot of people here who aren't Scots. Most of the incomers are from Yorkshire, though, and the northern accent doesn't seem to get up people's noses like my London one does.

To be honest, my first year here has been hell. Maybe things will be different now, but I'd come to dread getting on that bus in the mornings to go to school. Ross Bailey who lives in the only other house that's near ours never talks about anything except computers, and the others who get on along the way all know each other as if they were one big family. They natter on about people I don't know and things they've done that I've had no part in, and the whole thing has been really miserable. It got so bad that Mum dreamed up the idea of sending me off to a residential school on the mainland. She talked Dad into letting me sit the scholarship exam, and he took me over there three weeks ago. Braeforth, it's called, all rhododendron bushes and lawns. I'd be a weekly boarder, like Barney is at his Special School.

"It's all right for us." Mum was still hammering away at Dad's resistance. "Running the shop, we're never short of company. People are in and out all day, and they're so glad to have their local shop open again after all that time without it, they make us feel very welcome. But it's different for Fran."

I looked suitably woe-begone, and Dad shifted uncomfortably in his chair and said, "I know it hasn't been easy."

"Well, then," said Mum.

Dad reached for the newspaper and had another look at it. "At least they pay a living allowance," he said. He was weakening I could see.

"Of course they do," Mum said. "They're not asking for charity."

We couldn't have afforded charity, to be honest. Buying the shop took up all the money Dad got when Gran died, and more besides. I turned up the mute appeal, trying to look like a trodden-on spaniel, and Dad sighed and gave in.

"Oh, all right. If you're sure you want to risk it."

Dad's a bit wary of children. He was a teacher when we lived in London, and it left him sort of shell-shocked. I'd have thought he was quite good at

5

it, because he's kind, really, but he said what with the paperwork and the hooligans, it got too much.

Barney was clapping his hands again, dead chuffed that something nice was going to happen, though he didn't know what. Mum was clearing away the dishes with that little smile she has when she's got her own way – and I was grinning from ear to ear. A real friend all of my own for a whole week was going to be just brilliant.

After that, letters were written and forms were filled in, and it was all fixed up. Della Thomson, who was almost thirteen, like me, would be arriving on Saturday, July 15th, to stay with us for seven days. I dreamed about it constantly, and badgered Dad into buying an old chest of drawers at the Harbour Trust auction and painting it white, so that Della would have somewhere to keep her things. Mum read out a few details from the letter she'd got from the Holiday Scheme people. "Father unemployed, mother died five years ago, younger sister aged six . . ."

I wasn't listening, not really. None of that had much to do with the friend who was so real in my imagination. When she arrived, we'd make up for whatever bad time she'd had, and none of it would matter. The thought of her visit kept me going all through the summer term, and I even started to talk about Della Thomson to the people at school. They looked a bit surprised – they weren't used to me talking much. I'd become rather silent, I suppose, and maybe they thought I was standoffish. But all that would change on July 15th. I couldn't wait.

Two

Who'd have thought the weather could be so awful in the middle of July? This huge storm blew up, and the sea went wild, hurling seaweed and stones across the road as if some devil had got into it. On the Saturday morning when Della was to arrive, rain was lashing down out of a dark grey sky, and the wind was so strong that we weren't sure if the ferry would run. I had my fingers crossed – I'd have crossed my toes if I could – and Dad phoned the Pier to find out what was happening.

It was all right. The boat was on its way, they said, though it might be a bit late because they'd had a bit of difficulty loading the cars. So off we went, driving across the hill with the windscreen wipers going double speed against the rain, and down the winding road into Garvick. The boat was late, as they'd said, but at last it came pitching through the rough sea and slowly edged its way into its berth. Ropes came snaking down to be looped over the bollards, but even when the ramp was down and cars started to come off, the ferry was rolling gently, making the gangplank shift to and fro and the ropes creak.

Barney was holding Dad's big golf umbrella over us, laughing when the wind nearly dragged it out of his hand. Drips flew everywhere, a lot of them down our necks, but he was having a great time. He loves being in charge of anything. Dad spotted a couple of dull people he knows from the Natural History Society – at least, *I* think they're dull – and went off to talk to them. I think he was dodging Barney's drips.

"Those are the Duncans," Mum said, nodding in the direction of the dull couple. "They're having a holiday girl as well."

I said, "Are they?" I wasn't really listening. People had started to come down the gangplank, and I was trying to guess which of the various girls would turn out to be Della Thomson.

"Theirs is called Kerry McGuire," Mum said.

"Mmm." It was mostly families coming off the boat, or groups doing something outdoorish, in cagouls and boots, with huge rucksacks.

"There they are," said Mum, and waved.

A woman coming down the gangplank was holding up a bit of cardboard with something written on it, like they do at airports to meet people coming off planes, only the letters had run in the rain and you couldn't see what they said. I don't know how Mum knew who she was, but she was right. Two girls were following the wet-cardboard woman, and I stared at them, desperate to know which one was Della. I hoped it was the big, cheerful-looking one with the friendly face, because the other one looked sort of ratty and thin and thoroughly fed up.

The cardboard woman came and introduced herself, and the friendly girl smiled at me. I smiled back. My fingers were crossed again.

"This is Kerry," the woman said, with her hand on the friendly girl's arm. "And she is staying with Mr and Mrs Duncan."

Oh, no.

Kerry shook hands politely with her hosts, and Mr Duncan took her case and said, "Better get you home out of this rain."

I hoped my disappointment didn't show. I smiled at the ratty-looking girl, but she didn't smile back. She was wearing a black leather jacket with fringes, a lot too big for her, a short black skirt that only just showed below the jacket, black tights and black, clumpy shoes. Her hair was a strange beetroot colour, hanging in dripping spikes, and she carried a kiddy-type small rucksack shaped like Mickey Mouse, with round, plastic ears. Her face was deathly white, and she wore so much mascara that she looked like a panda.

"And this is Della," said the woman brightly. The Duncans were walking away to their car with Kerry McGuire.

The ratty-looking girl shot her a glance and muttered, "Del."

I said, "Hi, Del," and tried not to notice the look Dad gave Mum.

A beetroot streak was running down the side of the girl's face, and she rubbed at it with the sleeve of her leather jacket She was wearing big hoop earrings. Mum says I can't have my ears pierced until I'm sixteen.

Dad said heartily, "Right, Del – we're parked over there by the Tourist Office. Is that all the luggage you've got?"

"Yeah," said Del.

The cardboard woman, who had never stopped smiling, said, "Now, you do have my telephone number, don't you? Feel free to contact me any time if there are problems – but I'm sure there won't be. Have a lovely time, Della – I'll see you next Saturday."

Del nodded glumly. We started to move off through the puddles, and Barney put his hand on her arm and said, "Hi!"

She looked at his beaming face carefully. "Hi," she said, "How're you doin'?"

"I'm Barney," said Barney, and kept chattering while we walked over to the car and got in it. He was the only one of us who liked her from the start.

I sat between the girl and Barney on the back seat, which is awkward because you don't know which side of the hump in the floor to put your feet.

"Was it a rough crossing?" Mum asked over her shoulder. Silly question.

"Aye. Hellish."

"Were you sick?"

"Thought I was gonnae die." She sounded very Glasgow.

We all stared out at the wind-swept moor. After a bit, Dad cleared his throat and said, "Sorry the place isn't looking its best. It can be lovely when the sun's out."

Del didn't say anything.

After another mile or so, Mum turned round with her brightest smile and said, "We're going over to the other side of the island, to Carrach, which is where we live. It's quite a small village. You'll see the sea again in a minute, only it's – um – the other side."

Del nodded. After a few minutes, she said, "Is there amusements?"

"What sort of amusements?"

"Like, Alton Towers and stuff. We went once, the school took us. It was great."

Mum looked worried. "Well, no, not really. There's a slide and a couple of swings by the harbour. And in August a travelling fair comes sometimes – bouncy castle, that sort of thing. For little ones, really. Only last year some of the holiday cottage people complained about the noise, so I don't think they're coming again."

Del gave another small nod. She didn't say anything else. When we stopped outside our house, she got out and slung her Mickey Mouse bag over her shoulder and just stood there, waiting for whatever happened next. She was putting up with it, but she certainly wasn't enjoying it.

I suppose the place must have looked a bit depressing. The sea was still crashing over the rocks, and the grey sky seemed absolutely full of rain – and our little slate-roofed house with the shop next to it isn't a bit like Alton Towers. Apart from the Baileys' cottage next door, we're in the middle of nowhere. You'd never think the village was so close, because the road curves round past the big rocks and you can't see any other houses.

The light was on in Ross Bailey's bedroom where he has his computer, and I saw him look round the edge of the screen when we got out of the car. He didn't wave or anything, just glanced out then got on with what he was doing. He's always like that – can't wait to log on or whatever it's called, as if he has a different world and the ordinary one doesn't matter. He makes me so cross. At least, he did until a couple of days ago. Things may be different now.

We took our wet things off in the kitchen, and Mum fussed around, making coffee and getting Barney to put his boots away and asking Del if her feet were wet.

"They're okay," Del said.

I was still thinking about Ross, so I asked her, "Do you like computers?"

She shrugged and said, "Don't know, really."

I couldn't think of anything else to talk about, so I went on, "I'm not keen on them. I mean, I can see they're useful, but they're not *real*, are they?"

It was a totally stupid thing to say, but sometimes

if there are lots of things buzzing about in your head, you only manage to get hold of one of them, and the words leave out all the rest. I meant that Ross up there with his screen seemed to have an interest that was quite different from the rain and the sea and wet feet and wanting friends – but as it was, Del looked at me as if I was mad.

"Fran, why don't you take Del upstairs and show her where everything is?" Mum said, then added to Del, "You don't mind sharing with Fran, do you? It's a nice, big room."

" 'S all right," said Del. "They said I would."

I'd done a massive tidy-up. There was nothing lying about on the floor, and Mum had bought matching duvet covers for my bed and the spare one so they looked properly twinned, and the white-painted chest of drawers even had a vase of flowers on it.

"Dead posh," Del said. She sat down on the bed, gazing round. I thought she'd bounce a bit, the way you do on a strange bed, trying the springs, but she didn't, just sat still. She looked a bit weird, really. The beetroot-coloured hair had run even more, and so had her mascara, leaving a blur of black under her eyes. She caught me looking at her, and said, "What you staring at?"

I blushed. I blush horribly easily – it's really embarrassing "I was wondering who does your hair," I said, which seemed the politest way of putting it.

"My auntie. She's trained and everything – she works in Cathcart. She does mine for free. D'you like it?"

"Mmm." Del's hair was short at the back, but on top it was cut into these long spikes that fell all over the place.

"She could do yours," Del said. "She wouldnae charge if she knew you were my friend. You'd need to come to Glasgow but."

I said, "I'll think about it," and Del shrugged and said, "Just a suggestion. You don't have to."

Mum would have a fit if I had my hair like Del's. Mine is fairish and quite long, and it's usually in a pony-tail. I suppose it makes me look a bit young – maybe I'll do something different with it soon.

I said, "This chest of drawers is for you." I slid the drawers open, showing her that they were empty. Mum had lined them with wallpaper left over from when we did the living room.

"Thanks." Del stood up and pulled the string of her Mickey Mouse bag undone. She hauled out various tops and black tights and another very short skirt, and a nightie with a picture of two kittens on it.

"That's nice," I said.

"Aye." Del held the nightie up against her. "My gran gave it me to come away." It looked very white and new compared with the rest of her stuff.

"We've got two cats," I said.

Del perked up. "Have you? Where are they?"

"In the kitchen, I expect. They don't like going out in the rain. They're supposed to be for keeping the mice out of the shop."

"That your shop where we parked?"

"Yes. There's a door through to it from our kitchen."

"What's it sell?"

It was my turn to shrug. "Bit of everything, really. Groceries and sweets and cigarettes, papers and magazines, birthday cards, all that sort of thing. We do video hire, too, and animal feed – chicken pellets, pony nuts. Dog meal. And it's the Post Office as well. Mum does that usually, but Mrs McKinnon comes in if there's something special, like today." I tried not to think that today was turning out much less special than I'd hoped.

Del was putting her things into the chest of drawers. There weren't many of them. A thick felt-tip pen fell from among a tangle of tights and rolled across the floor, and she stooped for it quickly and put it back in her bag. I asked her if she liked drawing, and she said, "Sort of."

"I do," I said. There wasn't much I liked at Broray High, but the Art lessons were great. "Mrs Laidlaw – she's our Art teacher – wants us to do pictures of the houses on the island, specially the old ones like this. It's for a project called Our Vanishing Heritage."

Del obviously wasn't interested in heritages. She pushed the drawers shut, then sat down on her bed again. "Who looks after your brother?" she asked.

"Barney? Well – we do."

"Aye, but if your mum does the Post Office and you're at school—"

"He's away during term time. He goes to a Special School on the mainland, just comes home for the weekends."

"Does he like it?"

"Yes, I think so. They do lots of workshop things, and he likes being useful, it makes him feel important." I almost told her that I might be going to school on the mainland as well, but I didn't, not then. Braeforth, with its gravel drive and tennis courts and no boys, suddenly seemed so extremely posh that I blushed even to think of it.

"What about in the holidays?" asked Del.

"Holidays? Oh, Barney – well, he helps in the shop a bit, and he does these electronic game things. They keep him happy for hours. He comes to show you when he's won the fight or the race or whatever it is. It's real to him, he thinks he's really won."

How odd, I thought, that Barney and Ross could take the same pleasure in the screen world although there are so many things Barney can't do and so many that Ross can. Ross is really clever. They love him at school, because he gets everything right, and he's polite and charming with it. Makes you sick.

"Can we go downstairs?" said Del. "I want to see your cats."

Danny and Bimbo were curled up on their old blanket in front of the Rayburn. They're both tabby, but Bimbo has a white paw and Danny doesn't. Del knelt down beside them and did lots of stroking and crooning. "You're lovely, so you are. Just lovely." She seemed really keen on them. She looked up and asked, "Are they brothers?"

"Yes, they're from the same litter. We had them as kittens. Do you have a cat?"

Del shook her head. "Dad doesnae like animals."

"My dad doesn't, either, not really. Danny and

Bimbo aren't allowed in the living room or anything. He says they're working cats. Mum says he has to be joking."

"Your dad's all right," said Del, and went on stroking Bimbo.

Mum came in through the door to the shop and said, "Oh, there you are. How are you feeling, Del? Any better? Are you hungry?"

"Starving," said Del. "Could I get a packet of crisps from your shop?"

Mum doesn't hold with eating between meals, and she said, "We'll be having lunch soon." Then she relented and added, "You can have some crisps, though – tell Jim I said you could."

Del said, "I'll get some money." She started towards the stairs, but Mum laughed and said she'd stand her a packet of crisps, so we went through into the shop. It's a bit old-fashioned, even though Dad put in self-service shelves and wire baskets when we came. It still has sacks of wheat and stuff on pallets in the middle of the floor – and we don't have a huge range of crisps. Del wanted tandoori flavour, but she had to settle for salt and vinegar. She had cat-hair all over her skirt, but she didn't seem bothered.

Three

After lunch, Del went on playing with Danny and Bimbo. She made them chase a crisp bag for so long that they curled up and went to sleep, but even then, she kept stroking them and tickling their ears, and at last Danny got fed up and scratched her. Del went off, sucking her hand. I asked her if she needed a plaster, but she shook her head.

Mum and Dad were having quiet discussions about how to spend the afternoon. I suppose they'd assumed that I'd take Del out and show her the beach and everything, but it was much too wet for that. So Mum phoned Mrs McKinnon to mind the shop again, and we all set out in the car to the museum at Garvick.

Our museum isn't like the huge London ones that have dinosaur skeletons and Egyptian gods. It's housed in a low, whitewashed building that used to be a farm cottage, and it's really very small. Once all five of us were in the little upstairs room that has the photos of paddle steamers in it, we more or less filled it. Barney was taking up more space than usual, because he'd got excited about the steamers and so he was paddling his hands round and round and making engine noises. Some other people came in, but when they saw Barney they went out again. They often do that.

Del found a glass case on the landing, with medical stuff in it. There was an old photo of a doctor in a deerstalker hat, driving a horse and trap, and underneath was a leather bag full of horrendous instruments. Del was turning her head to read all the labels, and she seemed fascinated.

"*Obstetrical forceps*," I read. "And just look at those scalpels. Gruesome."

"It's no' gruesome," said Del. "It's interesting."

Dad came to join us and said, "You fancy being a doctor, Del?"

Del gave him a look as if he was being silly and said, "It's just I think surgery's great. My wee sister had a hole in her heart when she was born. They said at the hospital she'd to get an operation when she was a bit bigger, but they werenae sure it would work."

I said, "And did it?"

Del nodded. "Aye, it was great. It looked terrible at first – she'd this red scar right down the middle of her wee chest, and you could see all the stitch marks, but it's faded now. It just looks like a silver line."

I tried to imagine what it must have been like, having that happening to your baby, and said, "Your mum must have been worried sick."

Del nodded again but didn't say anything, and Dad gave me a shocked stare – then I remembered, and went hot all over. Del's mum had died. It had said so in the letter from the Holiday Scheme, Mum had read it out. How could I have forgotten?

Dad said cheerfully, "There's a great career for you, Del, being a surgeon."

"No' me," said Del.

"Yes, you could. You can do anything if you want to enough."

She shot him one of her looks, and made no reply. Trying to make up for my awful clanger, I said, "Well, someone's got to. I mean, the grown-up people get older and retire, and then it's our turn."

Personally, I'd hate to be a doctor. I can't think of anything worse than being shut up in some stuffy surgery with a lot of not-well people. Horrible, having to ask them to take their clothes off and then listen to their chests and look in their ears and their mouths. It's not that I'm squeamish, but I like to be outside, with space round me.

I can't believe this when I look back, but five minutes after that conversation over the medical stuff, in the same little museum, I found what I really would like to do. It was quite weird, as if something unfolded in a perfectly natural way. Mum took Barney off downstairs so that other people could come in and look at the paddle steamers, and I went too. Del was still hanging around over the surgical instruments, and Dad stayed with her. We'd seen the other stuff downstairs, but the one thing left was the smithy, across the cobbled yard. Being a Saturday, they were having a farriery demonstration.

Blue smoke drifted out from under the roof, and I sniffed and liked the smell – but I didn't expect the full-scale excitement that was waiting. I could see the hindquarters of a brown horse round the edge of the open door, and when I went in, the farrier was lifting a red-hot shoe off the forge with a long pair of tongs. He took it across to the horse and stooped to pick up a hind hoof and tuck it between his knees, in the slit between the two halves of his leather apron. With a great hiss of smoke, he tried the shoe against the hoof, then took the shoe across to the anvil and gave it a few ringing clouts with a hammer. He nodded when he tried it again, and explained to the watching gaggle of people that it was a good fit now. He dunked the shoe in a water bath, sending up a cloud of steam, then started to nail it on. Tap-tap, tap-tap, a light, dry sound, quite unlike the ring of iron on iron. When the point of each nail came through the outside of the hoof, he twisted it over with the claw end of the hammer and flattened it down.

Someone asked, "Doesn't it hurt?"

The farrier laughed. "Think he'd stand there and let me do this if it hurt?" Tap-tap, tap-tap. "Got to get it right, mind. Too near the edge, and the hoof will break away. Too far in, you'll hit the sensitive part."

Del came in behind me and said, "Ugh, what's that smell?"

"Horse," I said. "And hoof, and hot metal. Isn't it lovely?" I could have stood there all day, breathing it in. And that's when I knew this was what I wanted to do, mad though it seemed.

Del said, "They've postcards in that shop bit at the entrance. I'm goin' to get one for my sister, okay?"

"Okay."

The farrier was knocking another shoe into shape on the anvil. It glowed a pinky-red colour, and sparks were flying. When he brought it round to the other side of the horse, he passed quite close to me, and I said, "Can girls do that?"

I was so afraid he'd laugh, but he didn't. He glanced up as he stooped to fit the shoe, and said, "Aye, there's quite a few in the trade now. There's a lassie up in Inverness doing well. It's not easy to get an apprenticeship, though." He walked past again, dunked the shoe and added through the cloud of steam, "You'll need to be determined."

My face was red with excitement and the fire. "I will be," I said.

Nobody knows about it yet. Mum had her hands full that afternoon, keeping Barney out of harm's way from the forge, so she didn't hear my question to the farrier. Neither did Dad, because he'd gone to keep an eye on Del. It's a secret that I'm hugging close, but it's already giving a new shape to everything

The farrier threw out a few scraps of advice as he worked. "You'll need biology, so make sure you do that at school. Metalwork, too. And if there's anyone round you keeps horses, see if you can lend a hand. Get used to them, if you're not already."

26

Mum was approaching, with Barney in tow. "Better go, I think," she said. "He's getting a bit overexcited."

Oh, and so was I. I still am, whenever I think about it. "Best of luck," the farrier said when I turned to leave. I'll need it.

Four

Del was very odd about food. On that first day, she hardly ate anything at lunchtime, and Mum said, "That's the crisps." I thought she probably didn't like salad – lots of people don't. But when we got back from the museum, Del only fiddled about with the pasta Mum did for tea, and said she wasn't really hungry, and afterwards, she asked if she could have a Mars bar from the shop.

On Sunday mornings we take our time over breakfast because the shop's shut and there's no hurry. Dad always has bacon and egg, and I do, too, sometimes. Barney eats anything he can get hold of, at any time. He's a bit fat, really, but he wouldn't understand about diets, and it seems so unkind to refuse him what he wants. Del had a cup of tea and a bit of toast.

Mum said, "Wouldn't you like some fruit juice?"

"No, thanks."

"Yoghurt, then? Muesli?"

Del shook her head. Her hair looked even weirder today, because she'd gelled it into stiffer spikes, like an overgrown purple hedgehog.

"Well, what do you usually have?" Mum asked.

Del shrugged and said, "I go to the club sometimes, but it's twenty-five pence."

"What club?"

"Breakfast club. They have it at school. Cocoa and toast and cereal. Fruit an' that."

"We've plenty of cereal," Mum said. "What about those little individual packs?"

"Don't mind."

I'm never allowed the unhealthy sorts of cereal, but Mum trotted off into the shop and came back with one of those variety packs, and didn't bat an eyelid when Del went for the Coco Pops. Even so, it wasn't much of a success. Del ate about half of it, then said, "Can I give this to the cats?" Bimbo was a bit surprised, but Danny mopped it all up – he's a terrible pig.

"What *do* you like?" Mum asked.

"Anything, really," said Del. "Cheeseburgers. Pizza. Spaghetti bol."

"You didn't like the pasta last night."

"It had mushrooms in."

"Oh."

Lunch was no better, because Mum did quiche, with more salad, and you could see Del hated it. There was chocolate mousse afterwards, and she ate that, but I could see Mum looking sort of grim. She has firm ideas about food.

It was still raining, so Dad took Del and me on a guided tour of the distillery. Mum said she had things to do, and Barney was carefully sorting a box of oranges in the shop, looking for any bad ones, so he was quite happy. Dad offered to stay and look after him if Mum would rather go to the distillery but she gave him one of her looks and said, "No, thank you."

Dad had obviously drawn the short straw, but he was very good about it. He said he'd never been to the distillery (which was true) and had always wanted to see round it (which probably wasn't.) But anyway, off we went.

Del trailed after us past all the vats and pipes and huge tanks, and when Dad asked her what she thought of it, she said, "It smells like sick." So Dad gave up, and suggested a cup of tea in the cafeteria.

Pushing a tray past the glass shelves, Del said, "Could I get a beefburger? I'll pay for it."

Dad told her to put her money away, of course she could have a beefburger, and did she want anything else?

"Crisps," said Del. "And a Coke, please."

I had apple juice and a bit of shortbread, and Dad had coffee. When he was halfway through it, he looked at Del and said, "So you're not keen on this place?"

Del shook her head. "Whisky's awful," she said.

I said I'd never tasted it, but I'd tried sherry at Christmas and that was quite nice. She gave me a pitying glance and said, "It's no' the taste."

"What is it, then?" Dad asked.

"People get bevvied, don't they."

I wasn't sure what she meant. "Drunk?"

"Aye. Guttered. Legless."

"Can happen," Dad agreed.

Del took another bite of her beefburger, but I could see she'd gone off it. After a few moments, she put it down and pushed the plate away.

"Had enough?" Dad asked.

"Yes, thanks." Her face had gone tight and guarded. Something had gone wrong, but I didn't know what it was. Dad must have been feeling the same, because he asked her if she was okay.

"Fine," Del said. She drained her glass of Coke,

31

then pushed the unopened packet of crisps into the pocket of her leather jacket as we all stood up to go. But she wasn't fine, I thought. No way.

When we got home, Del turned the television on and sprawled on the sofa in the sitting room, eating the crisps she'd brought from the distillery.

I fidgeted about, perched on a chair by the window. I hate watching TV when it's daylight. Outside, rain was still drifting thinly past, though a watery sun was gleaming through a crack in the clouds. As I watched, a rainbow started to appear, the way they so often do here. It blossomed into a real beauty, a double arc that was very bright against the dark mass of cloud on the horizon, and it looked so close that you'd think the end of it was just across the road, springing from a crock of gold somewhere among the rocks.

"Hey, Del, just look at this rainbow," I said.

She turned her head a fraction and said, "Great," then returned her attention to the screen.

I had a sudden, ominous ache of tears, but I managed to say casually, "I might go out and have a look at it." I hoped she'd get up and come too, but she didn't, just said, "Okay." So I left her sitting there.

It was all such a crushing disappointment. I'd looked forward for so long to a week of companionship, and ended up with nothing more than a new kind of loneliness, feeling a prat for not being sure what "bevvied" meant. I walked across the road to the rocks and the sheep-nibbled grass, and stood there with my hands pushed into the pockets of my denim jacket. The sun had disappeared again and the rainbow was fading. Over in the Baileys' house, the light went on in Ross's room as the sky darkened.

All right for Ross, I thought. In his efficient cyberworld, nobody sprawled in front of the telly, eating crisps as if you didn't exist. Nobody curled up in bed at night with a threadbare grey rabbit she tried to hide from your sight, pretending to be asleep so you couldn't talk to her. Ross was never short of talk in a brightly printed form where everything was clear and sensible – he never had to guess the meaning of a sideways glance or wonder what lay behind a closed, guarded face.

The rain grew heavier as I stood out there, and my thoughts grew more morbid. Ross wouldn't care about old-fashioned things like friends and rainbows. Maybe his was the world we'd all live in one of these days, and people wouldn't need to meet each other any more. There would by cyber-marriages where the husband and wife only knew each other through the Internet, endlessly exchanging love-messages. They could see each other on the screen, admire each other's looks and cleverness, never quarrel about what colour to paint the kitchen or how to bring up the children because they'd be cyber-children, wouldn't they? Virtual babies, the perfect little boys and girls of your wishing. No rudeness, no wet beds, nothing unplanned, nothing worrying. No Barneys. Such a perfect world.

The tears that had threatened suddenly overwhelmed me. My fists were clenched in my pockets, and rain mingled with the tears that were pouring down my face. Everything seemed filled with sadness, even the small purple flowers of the thrift that grew in clefts between the rocks, even the gull that stood a little way off, shuffling its folded wings into neatness and watching me with a round, yellow eye.

Del might be watching through the window. It didn't seem likely, as she was less interested in me than the gull was, but the thought made me break into a clumsy trot, to get out of sight. I slipped on the brown seaweed thrown up by the storm, and my foot went down into the wet crack between the grass. *Careful*, a part of my mind said. *Don't be silly*. I crossed the road a bit farther down, past the Baileys' house, and came back along the grass verge. The shop stands between our house and the Baileys', and I skirted round behind it to go in through the back door. Just in case anyone should be in the kitchen, I paused outside to blow my nose on a rather grubby tissue – and Dad's voice drifted clearly through the fanlight of the storeroom behind the shop.

"Oh, a dead failure. She hated it."

He was talking to Mum. "Why?" she asked.

"Seems to have a hang-up about booze. Said something about people getting drunk, then went all quiet."

"Well," Mum said, "it's hardly surprising, is it? After what Mrs Mountford said—"

Mrs Mountford? Oh, of course, the cardboard woman.

"– quite a heavy drinker," Mum was going on. "And with a father like that—"

I didn't want to hear any more. I opened the kitchen door and went in, and the words could no longer be heard.

Five

It had to be the Castle the next day, since the rain still hadn't stopped. We'd done the museum and the distillery, and there's nothing much else on Broray when the weather's bad. All right when it's fine, you can go hill-walking or knock balls about on the Garvick putting green or take a boat out, or there's pony trekking, only you have to book ahead for that because it's so popular with the visitors. But it wasn't fine, it was dull and drizzly. So off we went again, Mum's turn on duty this time, with me beside her in the car, and Del and Barney in the back.

We got to the Castle car park, and then had trouble with Barney. He'd brought his Game Boy with him, and he wouldn't get out until he'd finished the boxing match. He sat there with his thumbs pushing the buttons like mad while the little figures on the screen ducked and bobbed and battered each other, with lots of ker-pow noises. The windows steamed up, and Mum said to Del and me, "You two go on into the Visitor Centre if you like, it's better than sitting here. I'll wait for Barney." It's never any good arguing with him, he just doesn't see his little boxers aren't real to other people, and he gets furious if you try to make him stop the game. It would be all right if he could manage to do his boxing-match and walk at the same time, but he can't – he always trips over or collides with things. So you just have to wait.

Del and I got out of the car and climbed the wooden steps to the Visitor Centre. They only built it last year – people say there used to be bluebell woods here before. Tourists like it, though, because it's full of stuff like bird-watching books and table-mats with pictures of thistles on them. There's a big range of jokey T-shirts, as well, with slogans on them like *Broray University* and *I met the Midges and Survived* – and guess who was standing there, smiling over them as if they were really witty? Kerry McGuire, with the dull Duncans. She waved when she saw us, beaming all over her face, and said, "Hi, Del!"

"Hi," said Del.

"Isn't it brilliant!" Kerry said. "I'm having a great time, are you?"

" 'S all right," said Del. "Bit boring."

I could have killed her. We'd been turning ourselves inside out to try and amuse her, and that's all she could say. The Duncans did their best to smooth it over, wittering on about the weather and saying how much better the forecast was now. Mrs Duncan said, "We're going on the *Waverley* tomorrow. It's an old paddle steamer, the last one left."

I'd been on the *Waverley* last summer, and it was great, so I tried to look very encouraging, hoping the Duncans would offer to take us, too. And they did. Mr Duncan said, "You'd be most welcome to join us, unless you have other plans."

Del said flatly, "No, thanks. That boat we came on was hellish."

The Duncans nodded and looked a bit wall-eyed, and Kerry kept on smiling. Mrs Duncan said, "Well, have a lovely time, anyway. The Castle's nice, isn't it?"

I said, "We haven't been in yet, we're waiting for Mum."

There were more nods and smiles. "You'll adore it," Mrs Duncan told Del. "So interesting."

Del didn't adore it, of course. The stags' heads all the way up the staircase put her off, for a start. "That's horrible," she said. "Fancy shooting all those poor things." I could have told her it was better than being packed into a lorry and sent off to a slaughterhouse, but I thought I'd better not.

We went on through rooms with huge double beds in them, and when we came to a dressing room at the end, Del sat down on a gilt sofa. A woman with an Official Guide badge told her to get up, because it was an exhibit. Del got up, scowling, and shifted across to the window seat. "This all right?" she asked.

"Yes, you can sit there," the woman said, and added merrily, "Goodness, you young people don't have the use of your legs these days!"

Del had the sense to ignore this. She stared out at the cedar trees and the sloping lawns that run down to the sea, and said, "Does one person own all this?"

"One family used to," the woman said, looking pleased at finding a sucker for some history. She started a lot of stuff about the Dukes of Hamilton, but Del wasn't on for that. "How did they get it, then?" she asked.

"It was inherited. Handed from father to son over many years."

"Aye, but how did they get it in the first place?"

"They built it."

"But what about all this?" Del waved a hand at the cedar trees.

"They owned the land, naturally. At that time, they owned the whole island. They were the ruling family."

Del shrugged and gave up, but I could see what she was driving at, so I said, "How does a family come to rule?"

"There were various battles," the guide said rather stiffly. "So the winners of course lay claim to the land."

Del and I exchanged glances and almost smiled. "There you go, then," Del said. "They just took it. All right for some."

The guide breathed in very patiently and said, "Why don't you move on to the sitting room? And do keep off the furniture, won't you?"

There was a group of visitors in the corner of the sitting room, which was enormous, looking at a picture of a man on a horse and listening to a lecture from a woman who wore glasses with a little chain round the back. Mum was on the outskirts with Barney, trying to hush him because he'd got excited about the horse. The guide in this room was a man in a kilt, standing in the far doorway with his arms folded, keeping a stern eye on Barney.

Del wandered across to look at a writing desk with lots of little drawers – and the next minute, a shrieking electronic bleeper went off, and the man in a kilt leapt half out of his skin. He shot across to the desk and fished in one of its drawers for a key, and turned the noise off. The group by the picture turned to stare at us in the sudden silence, and the kilted man glared at Del and said, "Somebody must have touched it. It's alarmed."

"No' half as alarmed as he was," Del muttered in my ear. "Did you see him jump!"

We both giggled, and everyone looked at us as if we were a nasty smell. Barney started laughing and clapping his hands and making alarm noises, and Mum said we'd better go and look at the kitchens. She took us off along musty corridors and down a lot of stone steps to this great barn of a place full of copper pans, and tried to get us interested in a knife sharpener. It was no good. Once you've got the giggles, everything seems funny, and the knife-sharpener simply set us off again. And that's when I knew I could like Del. Really and truly like her.

Six

The Duncans were right about the weather. The next morning, it was bright and clear.

Mum and Dad seemed relieved. "Maybe you two would like to go somewhere on your own," Mum said to Del and me. Dad suggested a bike ride. Del could take Mum's if we put the seat down a bit – but Del said, "Bikes give me a sore bum." So that was that.

There was silence round the breakfast table, and Mum said, "Well, I don't know."

Unexpectedly, Del said, "Is there a bus?"

Everyone brightened at once. Mum said, "Oh, yes, they go over to meet the boats, so there's five a day. And if you fancied it, you could go on the Open-Top Experience to Black Rocks Bay. People say it shoogles a lot, but you get a lovely view." You'd never think Dad was the Scottish one of the pair, the way

Mum throws in odd words like "shoogles". If we went to Australia, she'd be the first one to start calling people "sport".

Del wasn't keen on the Open-Top Experience. "I'm no' bothered," she said. I suppose they have open-top tour buses in Glasgow.

"What are you going to do, then?" Dad asked.

Del shrugged and said, "Look round the shops and that. There might be a jumble sale." She was much more talkative today. "They're great, jumble sales. See my leather jacket? I got that for twenty pee."

"Our jumble sales are always on a Saturday, because people are working in the week," Mum said. "There's the BRAR shop, though."

"I'm no' wantin' a bra," said Del.

I explained that it stood for Broray Rheumatism and Arthritis Research. "It's a charity shop."

"Dead expensive, most of those," Del said. "It's no' important. Just – you know – look around a bit."

I got the feeling that she wanted things to be ordinary. For the last three days we'd been knocking ourselves out, trying to do the hospitality bit, and I suppose it had got kind of heavy. Mum eventually accepted the idea that we didn't need a detailed plan for the day, but she was still in full mother-hen mode, and insisted on making us a packed lunch. There were questions about what Del liked in her sandwiches and whether we'd take apples or bananas or both, and a stream of advice on where the nicest walks were.

When all the food and the packs of juice were in a plastic carrier, Mum handed it to me and said, "Now, Fran, you will take care of Del, won't you? If you get fed up or the weather turns nasty, just phone, all right? One of us will come over and fetch you if you're between bus times. The Library's open in the afternoon, you could shelter there if it rains. You've got a phonecard, haven't you? And money?"

Out of the corner of my eye, I saw Del glance at the ceiling in exasperation, and I said, "Yes, all *right*, Mum. You don't have to fuss."

It was an awful moment. I'd never said anything like that to Mum before, not ever, and she gave me a long look that said more than words. I couldn't explain that I'd seen it from Del's point of view for a moment, that was all, so I just muttered, "Sorry." But as we went out to get the bus, I could still feel Mum looking at me.

Ross Bailey was waiting for the bus as well, with a duffel bag over his shoulder. I said, "Has the Internet shut down, then?" and he gave me his easy grin.

"Exercise time," he said. "Julie Crombie phoned, said I'd to come swimming with the gang. Mum took the call, unfortunately, and she's convinced my body will seize up with disuse, so she said I'd be there. No choice."

"Tough," said Del.

I did the introductions, and Ross shook hands politely. That's partly what everyone swoons over, those lovely manners. He's not a wimp, though. He was out in a dinghy in bad weather last year and the mast broke, but he'd got it all sorted out by the time the rescue people arrived.

"I saw you on Saturday," he said to Del. "Getting out of the car in pouring rain. Not the best of Broray's weather."

"Hellish," Del agreed. "I just wanted to die. If it hadnae been for having to get on that boat again, I'd have gone home."

I was gobsmacked. Here she was, telling a total stranger about how miserable she'd been, and she'd never said a word to me. Perhaps she'd sensed that I was all stressed up, trying to make it work, and didn't want to tell me that she hated it. And now, she was chatting on to Ross as if she'd known him for years. "I never get a go on the school computers, the boys hog them all the time." Ross must have asked her if she was into all that – I hadn't been listening.

"There ought to be enough for everyone," Ross said. And off they went again, about schools and their electronic equipment. I couldn't find anything to say, so I just listened. Then I noticed that it was Ross who did most of the talking. When he paused, Del would say, "Is that right?" or "That's amazing," – and he'd be off again. For someone who'd shown no particular interest in computers when I'd asked if she liked them, she was putting up a good show of being absolutely fascinated.

More people got on the bus at its various stops, all of them going to Garvick, and we got off at the Pier with everyone else. Julie Crombie and the others were standing outside the craft shop with their swimming stuff, and they waved when they saw Ross. I wished they were waving at me, too. I'm a good swimmer. What's more, Julie Crombie's parents run the pony-trekking centre. *Lend a hand*, the farrier had said. *Get used to horses*. Some hopes.

"See you around, Del," Ross said. "Enjoy the rest of your week. 'Bye, Fran." And he went off to join the others.

"Dead boring, isn't he?" said Del.

"*Boring*?" What on earth could she mean? "I

thought you liked him. You sounded so interested."

Del shrugged. "They always like you to sound interested," she said. "My dad's the same. If he's on about something, you've to look as if you're listening, else he goes ballistic."

"Sounds awful," I said. We were heading across to the craft shop, though I didn't particularly want to.

"No' really," said Del. "He just gets fed up. He's unemployed, see."

"My dad was unemployed for a bit," I said. "He gave up being a teacher, then there was a gap before we got the shop going."

"That's different," said Del. And I suppose she was right.

Ross and Julie and the others were still grouped round the door when we reached the craft shop, waiting for someone to come off the south-about bus, probably. Liz Marr said, "Hi, Fran," as we passed them and went in, and a couple of the others smiled.

I said, "Hi," because I'm always trying to be friendly, but Del didn't bother, just pushed through the door. And when we were both inside, she turned to face me and said, "Look, you don't have to stick with me all day."

I felt my face flush with the shock of it. I started to say it was no trouble, I actually liked being with her, but she cut me short. "I'm no' used to being nannied about," she said. "I just want to be on my own. Get it?"

Mum had said I was to look after her. "But I can't—"

"Yes, you can. Go and sketch your old houses or whatever. I'll see you later."

"Del, please – I mean, what are you going to do? Where shall we—"

"Over there by the buses. Three-ish. Go on, shove off." And she walked away and stared at the refrigerated display of Broray cheese.

I should have stuck with her, I know I should. I ought to have had it out with her there and then, and faced up to the row, if that's what it came to. But I didn't, I was too upset. I went out of the shop, trying not to cry, and the group outside stared at me with all its curious eyes. Someone said, "Where's your friend?"

"She's not my friend," I snapped. "She's just a visitor." And I kept walking.

Ross called after me, "Hey, Fran—" And Julie said, "What's the matter?"

I half wanted to go back, because that note of concern and friendliness was what I'd longed for, but I knew I'd burst into tears and the idea was too embarrassing, so I broke into a run, past the bus park and across the road then up the hill that led away from the town until I was out of breath and the crowd with its curiosity, friendly or not, was left behind.

I slowed down then, panting, and turned to look back. Nobody was following. The sea was very blue down there, and the departing ferry looked no bigger than a toy boat, tracing its curve of white wake as it headed off to the mainland. Over there behind that misty line of hills was the school I'd be going to if I'd passed the exam. I almost wished I was there now, walking among those other girls in their sage-green uniforms, away from all this muddle and difficulty.

The *Waverley* came chugging round the headland towards the berth the ferry had vacated. Even from so far up the hill, I could hear the splashy thumping of her engines. Kerry McGuire and the Duncans would be down there among the crowd waiting to go aboard. Del and I could have been there as well. It would have been such fun, with a jazz band playing and strings of flags flying, and all the dads down below, leaning on the brass rail and watching the huge shafts of the engine sliding to and fro. And instead, I was stuck here on my own for a whole day of awful emptiness.

For a moment, I wondered whether to phone Mum and tell her what had happened – but I couldn't do that. It would sound such a failure, and I'd already upset Mum once this morning. No, I'd have to stick it out here, and meet up with Del at three as she'd said. With any luck, nobody need know things had gone so wrong. The people from school knew, of course, but that was something else. I couldn't imagine what they'd think about it.

Go and sketch your old houses, Del had said. She'd seen me put my little sketchbook in my rucksack, I suppose, and thought she was in for hours of boredom while I scribbled. The stupid thing was, I probably wouldn't have used it at all, but Mrs Laidlaw had said the important thing is always to have your sketchbook with you, like a photographer always carries a camera. It's when you haven't got it that you see something interesting. And you don't properly know what things look like, she says, until you start to draw them.

Up there on the hill, there was nothing worth drawing. The houses were the modern sort, square and dull, with privet hedges and satellite dishes. If I really was going to spend the next few hours sketching my old houses – and there seemed to be nothing else to do – then this wasn't the place. I turned along a side road that ran parallel to the sea, and started to walk again.

The road led me back to the other end of Garvick, near the Post Office, but there were several ways up the hill from there. I went past the church and kept going, trying to look purposeful, and after a while the road petered out into a rough track, leading up between trees. There were horses in a field, and when they saw me they ambled over to see if I had anything for them. The bag with the packed lunches for me and Del was still in my rucksack, so I fished in it for an apple. Del wouldn't have eaten her apple anyway, even if she'd been here.

I tried hard not to think about how much I wished Del was here. Only yesterday, I'd been so sure I could like her, and even hoped she might like me a bit, and now she'd thrown all that away. I bit the apple into chunks and held them out, flat-handed, one at a time to the horses. The lovely smell of them was there again, and I patted the strong necks, feeling the warmth and roughness of them, as excited as I'd been in the smithy.

I fished my sketchbook out and spent the next half-hour or so trying to draw the horses. It was difficult to get a clear view of the ones that were near me, because half of them was hidden by the wall, but farther away, there was a mare with her foal. She wouldn't bring him close, but that was fine.

They were amazingly difficult to draw. The foal's legs were as long as his mother's, and his head was quite big, but the rest of him was baby-sized. I wasn't much better with the mare, to be honest. I kept getting her back end wrong, all balloony and shapeless. I couldn't work out how her hind leg joined up with her back. What I needed was one of those books with pictures of skeletons, so that I could work it out. Perhaps I might go down to the library and see if they had one. Not yet, though. If Del was looking round the shops, I might meet her, and that would be so embarrassing.

I went on past the trees and came to the buildings of an old farm, whitewashed and slate-roofed. Ideal. I hitched myself onto the stone wall and settled down to a more detailed drawing. When that one was finished, I did another, looking across to the byre and a big chestnut tree. My bum was getting numb from sitting on the rough wall, so I shoved the sketchbook back in my bag and set off again, up the hill. The track stopped at the farm, and after that there were just sheep-paths, skirting past boulders and thorn bushes. I was getting quite close to the open moor and the mountain, but I didn't want to go off up there. It would be crazy to risk getting lost – and besides, I was quite hungry. I found a dry, grassy place where I could sit with my back against a rock, and fished out Mum's sandwiches.

Del would be hungry, too. But was that my fault? She could have been here, sharing this picnic. I wished she was. I glanced at my watch. Ten past two. The hours had gone more easily than I'd hoped. Quite soon, I'd start walking back to meet Del. About three, she'd said – though she didn't have a watch, so I wasn't sure how she'd know. But she could ask, and there was a clock outside the Post Office, if she happened to be along that end.

It's funny how you never seem to take as long as you expect if you're not in a hurry. It was a bit less than two-thirty when I reached the Post Office, so I still had half an hour to kill. I started across the road towards the library.

There's something odd about drawing. When you've been doing it, you notice things much more, as if they'd somehow become extra distinct and brighter-coloured. The geraniums outside the tennis courts looked quite amazingly red, and the people moving about on the bowling green were as sharp as if they'd been performing on a stage. There were less pleasant things shouting to be noticed, as well – Irn Bru cans under the bushes, dog poo, crisp packets, graffiti. Not that we have a lot of graffiti, it's not all over the place like it is in Glasgow. But today, there seemed to be more. On the side of the phone box the was a blue, spray-canned sign, an upright stroke with a circle round it that didn't quite close on the left-hand side. The same mark was on the wall round the side of the chemist's shop, and on a B & B sign outside a guest-house where the fuchsia hedge almost reaches it.

I stopped and looked again, with a sudden, awful suspicion. The stroke in its open circle was terribly like a capital D. D for Del? No, I mustn't get paranoid about it – there were dozens of names that began with D – Don, Dave, Danny . . . boys' names, naturally enough. It must be a gang of boys who did this sort of thing. I went on into the library.

They had a book about animal skeletons, muscles, too. I couldn't borrow it, because I didn't have a ticket with me, but I looked carefully at the horse picture and the zig-zag way the bones in the hind leg went. I tried to concentrate really hard, so that I'd remember every detail, but my mind kept jumping off to fret about Del. It couldn't have been her doing those fuzzy-edged blue markings – she didn't have a spray can, I'd have seen it when she was putting things away in her chest of drawers. There had been the felt-tip marker, right enough. I'd asked if she liked drawing, and she'd said, "Sort of." What sort? Had I been stupid? Yes, probably. There was something about Della Thomson that made me feel an absolute idiot.

I put the horse book back on the shelf and went out into the sun. Walking past the ornamental flower beds, with the hotels and gift shops on the other side of the road, I tried not to look for Del, but somehow I was scanning every group of tourists, every pair of strolling girls, every solitary figure. And suddenly, there she was, sitting on the parapet of the bridge where the burn runs out into the sea, drinking a can of Coke. She saw me and waved cheerfully.

"Sorry about this morning," she said when I joined her. "I didnae mean to upset you."

" 'S all right." I sounded all bright and sensible like Mum, but I couldn't look at her.

"Hey." She reached out and put her hand on my arm. "C'mon."

After a bit of a struggle, I got everything under control and managed to ask, "Have you had a good day?"

"No' bad. I posted a card to Sylvie."

"Your sister?"

"Aye. And one to my gran, and my auntie. And Dad."

"I'm sorry about the packed lunch. It was in—"

"Doesnae matter."

"We could go out to Black Rocks Bay if you liked. There's still time."

"No, thanks."

So we went home.

Seven

On the bus, Del ate her half of the packed lunch, and even drank the carton of juice. She seemed in a much better temper.

"Did you do some drawing?" she asked.

I showed her the sketches, and she thought they were really good, specially the horses. She said, "I wish I could draw like that."

The questions I couldn't ask started rushing about in my mind. Draw like what? And if Del didn't do my sort of drawing, then what *did* she do? I said cautiously, "But I thought you liked art."

Del smiled and looked out of the window. "I'd like to do something really big," she said.

"Like, on a wall or something?"

She didn't answer, just went on looking out.

The writing on the wall. I didn't want to believe it. Maybe she meant something else. I tried again.

"Some of the tower blocks have paintings on the side. There was one near us in London – it was a street scene. You felt you could walk right into it."

"That where you come from, London?" Del asked.

"Yes."

"What made you come here, then?"

I started to explain about Gran dying and all the rest of it and how Dad came from a Scottish family, so he'd always thought of Scotland as home, and Del sounded so interested that it ended up with me doing the talking, all the way home. Every time I stopped she'd say something like, "So what happened after that?" – and I'd be off again. It wasn't until afterwards that I realised she'd done the same thing with me as she had with Ross, kept me talking and said nothing herself.

When we got off the bus outside our house, Ross himself came out and walked towards us, looking as if there was something he wanted to say. Since he and Del had got on so well this morning, I assumed he wanted to show her his computer or something, so I said, "See you," and was going on towards our door – but I'd got it wrong.

"Fran, wait," Ross said. He was blushing to the roots of his fair hair. I stared at him, and Del was the one who kept going, without a backward glance.

Ross couldn't meet my eye. "Look," he said, "this is awful, but I thought I'd better tell you, because you might wonder why I hadn't."

"What?" The lurking dreadfulness of the day suddenly gathered itself into a tight ball in my stomach.

"It's about Del. You know you came out of the shop without her and went off on your own – well, we were still there for a bit, waiting for Rachel and Kirsty to come off the other bus. Then Del came out and walked past, didn't say anything, and a few minutes after that, Mrs Murchie came rushing out, wanted to know if the girl with purple hair was with us. We said she wasn't, and Mrs Murchie said – I'm really sorry about this, Fran – she said Del had pinched a Talky Bear. One of those wee teddies with a voice that works on remote control. They're quite expensive, about ten pounds."

"Oh, no." I should have stayed – I could have prevented it.

"It's not your fault," Ross said. "I mean, you weren't there. But the thing is, Mrs Murchie saw you and Del together, and she knows who you are, so she said she's going to ring your dad."

She and Dad went to the same wholesaler on the mainland, they knew each other well. With a faint

60

flicker of hope, I said, "Is she sure it was Del? There were other people in the shop."

"She seemed pretty sure," said Ross. "We didn't know if it was best to tell you, but Julie said if it was her, she'd rather know."

"Yes." She was probably right, but either way, I was going to be in deep trouble. "Thanks, anyway," I said. "Better go and see what's happening, I suppose."

"Best of luck," said Ross.

Mum was waiting for me in the kitchen. She let me put my bag down, then said, "Now, what exactly has been going on?"

"Nothing. I—"

"Fran, don't give me that. You left Del on her own in the Pier craft shop. Didn't you?"

"Well, yes, but—"

"I can't understand you. She's our guest – *your* guest. She's a stranger to Broray, and you were supposed to be looking after her."

"She didn't want me to. She said—"

"I don't care what she said. She was your responsibility."

"I know." And in fact I didn't want to tell Mum what Del had said. In a rather hopeless way, I still wanted the visit to be a success, so I had to keep making out that she was all right.

"I'm really sorry," I said.

Mum sighed. "You know what happened, don't you?"

"Yes. Ross just told me."

There was a pause, then Mum went on, "I know she's difficult, Fran. Maybe the whole thing was a bit of a mistake, and I'm sorry if you're disappointed, but we've the rest of the week to get through – and we do have to try and see it from Del's point of view. She's used to living in a city, and things are very different there. Probably in Glasgow shops, valuable things are kept well out of reach. We're more relaxed here, we don't assume that people are going to steal. Perhaps we should do, it's only putting temptation in people's way..."

I nodded, but I wasn't really listening. *See it from Del's point of view?* I'd been desperate all this time to understand how she felt, and much good had it done me. Why a Talky Bear, of all things? I couldn't see that Del would be into electronic animals, she was too keen on the real thing. She was always trying to sneak Danny or Bimbo upstairs, though she knew they were supposed to stay in the kitchen. It just didn't seem like her.

"Is Mrs Murchie sure it was Del?" I asked, interrupting what Mum was saying. "There were other people in the shop, it could have been anyone."

"I asked her that when she phoned," Mum said. "But she'd seen Del fingering these things, and felt she should keep an eye on her. When you run a shop, you get this sense of who's up to no good. It's the same with us – there was a boy the other day. I knew he was trying to pinch a pack of fishing hooks and he did."

"Yes, but—"

"Mrs Murchie got called to the counter because a customer wanted new batteries in a camera – one of the helpless sort – so she dealt with that, and while she was busy she saw Del slip out. And the Talky Bear had gone."

"That doesn't prove—"

Mum lost patience. "Oh, don't be silly, Fran. It's no use kidding yourself. Your dad told Mrs Murchie we'll pay for the wretched thing – there's really no doubt that Del took it. He's very fed up. He says we should pack her off home."

"Oh, Mum, he mustn't!" To end it like this would be awful. And what's more, it would all be my fault.

"Don't worry," Mum said. "Once he's calmed down, he'll be all right. I don't think we should bale out at the first hiccup. And you never know, things may improve."

"Hope so."

Mum gave me a hug. "Sorry I was cross," she said. "But you can see why I was upset, can't you?"

I nodded miserably. I could see, all right. And she wasn't half as upset as I was.

Del was lying on her bed with her eyes closed, cuddling the threadbare grey rabbit. "So what was the matter wi' Ross?" she asked, with her eyes still shut.

I didn't answer. She rolled over and looked at me and said, "Well, come on."

The truth had to be told. "There's a Talky Bear missing from the Pier craft shop."

"And they think it was me," said Del. "Well, it's no', see."

I wanted to believe her, but I couldn't say anything.

"I knew that woman was watching me," Del went on. "Rotten old cow." After a few minutes, she asked, "What do *you* think?"

I felt my face go hot. I said, "I don't know, I wasn't there. If it wasn't you, fine." I'm such a coward, I simply couldn't say I thought she was a thief.

Del didn't say anything, just rolled away from me

again and curled up with her rabbit. I sat on the edge of my bed, and the silence between us grew and grew.

At last I couldn't bear it any more, so I got up and went out of the room, down to the shop to see if there was anything I could do. The dairy van had just come in – it takes them all day to get the morning's milk pasteurised and put in cartons – so I ended up helping Barney to bring the crates in. We stacked it all in the fridge, together with the cheese and the yoghurt.

Eight

At tea-time, we tried hard to be relaxed. Mum dished out raspberry ripple ice-cream after the fish fingers – which Del had eaten without complaint – and said cheerfully, "Who's for the ceilidh tonight?"

"Count me out," said Dad, but Mum gave him such a meaningful look that he coughed a bit and changed his mind. "Oh. Well, I suppose I can catch up on the accounts later."

"Video the football and catch up on *that* later, you mean," said Mum. "How about you, Del? Fancy your hand at Strip the Willow?"

"Don't mind," said Del.

So we all went, Barney too. His idea of dancing is a bit funny, but nobody minds. Everyone's used to him now, and he always has a great time. The ceilidh was in Carrach Village Hall. It's not very big, and it was quite crowded, because the Castle

Band were playing, and they're really good – drums and accordion and our school bus-driver on guitar. When I first came here, it seemed quite strange that people of all ages came to a dance, even quite young children, but I like it now. Ross was there, looking even more spruce and well-brushed than usual, in a kilt, and Rachel had come with her friends from the South End, and George from the dairy had set up his disco for in between the band sessions, so you could keep dancing, without a stop. Mum went off to help with the refreshments, because there was a bar and lots of home-baking as usual, and when Ross saw us he came over and asked Del to dance, which was pretty nice of him, I thought.

Mind you, Del looked amazing. She was wearing her shortest black skirt, which only just covered her bum, and a skinny top that showed a lot of midriff, and she'd washed her hair after tea, and gelled it into fresh spikes. It was a darker colour, though, because she hadn't been able to get any hair-dye of the right sort in Garvick, she said. She was a terrific dancer, too. I'm only just getting to know things like the Gay Gordons, but she'd obviously been doing them for years. She was great at disco dancing as well, so lots of other boys asked her after she'd danced with Ross, and she never sat down all evening.

I had quite a good time, too. I usually feel a bit awkward, and end up helping Mum to clear away dirty glasses or something, even though she always tells me to go and enjoy myself, but this time people kept coming up and asking who my friend was, and asking me to dance. It all seemed amazingly easy.

The sky was full of stars as we walked home along the shore road, and the moon was making a bright path across the sea.

"I can see why you like it here," Del said.

I was surprised. "I didn't think you were into it."

"Why?"

"You told Ross you thought it was hellish. You said you wanted to go straight home." My triumphant evening had made me feel a bit reckless. "And you told the Duncans it was boring."

"The who?"

"Those people Kerry McGuire's staying with."

"Oh, aye. Well, that was just at first. And I'm no' sayin' Broray's for me – just I can see why you like it."

"I didn't when I first came. Not for ages."

"How no'?"

68

"I just felt so strange, I suppose."

"You would," Del agreed. "I mean, you *were* strange, right?"

"Right." Put so simply, it made me feel a bit of a prat.

"Is there just one school on Broray?" Del asked.

"Just one secondary, yes. There's a primary school in each village."

"No' much choice, then."

"No." And before I knew it, I was telling her all about the plan to send me to Braeforth, and about the scholarship exam and the rhododendron bushes and the girls in their sage-green skirts and white blouses, strolling on the lawn.

"D'you think you'll like it?"

"I don't know." And I really didn't know. It had seemed such a haven of smiles and politeness at first. Its library had cushioned window-seats that looked as if people were supposed to curl up and browse in them, and there was a music room with a huge grand piano, and nothing was built of breeze block, and nobody carted black-and-purple sports bags about. But in spite of these things, when I thought of it now, the idea of getting on the boat every Sunday evening as Barney did during term-time, and going away to a mainland place where I wouldn't see the sea for a week, gave me a panicky feeling inside.

We walked the rest of the way home in silence. Perhaps I'd failed the scholarship exam. I almost hoped I had – it would rescue me from the awful choice that lay ahead. All else apart, I couldn't imagine that the teachers at Braeforth, in their beautifully tasteful skirts and jerseys, would take kindly to one of their girls becoming a farrier.

Once again, though, I'd been the one who did all the talking, and when we were back at home and in our beds after a late-night cup of tea, I said, "What's your school like?"

"No' bad," said Del. After a pause, she added, "They're gonnae close it."

"Why?"

"Save money. We've all to go to Northburn." She frowned. "Such a bummer."

"Maybe you'll like it when you get there," I said. And maybe I'd like Braeforth.

"It's no' about *liking* it," said Del. "I'm no' bothered where I go. Just, it's further."

"Takes longer to get there?"

"Aye." She was still frowning. "See, the way it is now, I drop my wee sister at her school then go on to mine, because it's just nearby, but at Northburn

I'll need to get the bus. And it's too early for Sylvie. And she cannae go alone, there's too many roads to cross."

"Can't your dad take her?"

"He's no' up in the mornings," Del said.

I nodded, trying to look as if I understood – but I didn't. If Del's father was unemployed, why couldn't he take his little daughter to school?

"He doesnae sleep much," said Del. "The doctor says he's depressed."

"Is he looking after Sylvie while you're here?"

"No, she's with my gran. She's only six, see, and you've to be seven to come on this Holiday thing. I was for turning it down when the letter came, but my gran and my auntie said go for it."

"Where does your gran live?"

"Govan." Del remembered that she was still wearing her earrings, and turned her head to take them out. She crawled along her bed to drop them on the chest of drawers, then got back under the duvet.

"That's on the river, isn't it?" I was trying hard to keep this conversation going. "My dad's father used to work in the shipyards, only he moved south when it all closed down."

"Aye, no' far." Del reached up to switch off her

bedside light, then turned on her side and snuggled down. " 'Night," she said.

So that was that.

Nine

"So what's the plan for today?" Dad asked at breakfast. He was being amazingly good, considering it was only yesterday that he'd been wanting to pack Del off home.

Del didn't say anything, and I said, "Haven't thought" – though in fact I seemed to have been thinking about it all night either awake or asleep. Several times, I'd woken in a fret, trying to decide what we could do, and then I'd be back in a weird dream about a boat trip. We were on the *Waverley*, and Del had covered the funnels with graffiti and then taken over command. She was standing at the wheel, wearing a captain's cap and a navy jacket with gold epaulettes, steering her way up the river to Govan, to collect Sylvie and her gran. The cats were there, too, and I was worried they might jump overboard and drown, but a sailor kept telling me it was all right. The captain was in charge, he said. But it was just a dream.

Mum said, "Why don't you go swimming? Did you bring a costume, Del?"

"Aye. My auntie gave me one, specially to come. Brand new, from Every's. I'm no' much good at swimming, though."

Mum wasn't to be put off. "But there's a Jacuzzi and a warm paddly pool," she said, "so you don't have to swim all the time. It's really nice, isn't it, Fran? It was only opened three years ago. Then in the afternoon you could play tennis, perhaps – you can hire rackets. Or have a go at the Crazy Golf or take a boat out."

"I'm not having these two out in a boat on their own," Dad said firmly. "No way. I'll take you if you want to go," he added to Del and me, "but–"

We both said not to bother about boats, then Del said, "Thanks, though, for offering." It was the first time she'd been that polite, and Mum and Dad both looked pleased.

"Or pony trekking," Mum went on. "I could phone and see–"

"No, thanks," said Del.

She was frowning a bit, and I thought as I had done yesterday that there was too much fuss. "We'll just go swimming," I said. "Then for a walk or something. Okay?"

Del said, "Okay," and I tried to look very responsible. Whatever we ended up doing today, I wouldn't let her out of my sight.

The swimming pool really is pretty good. "Dead posh," Del said when she first saw it. "Can anyone go in there?"

I knew how she felt. It's not a bit like the echoing Victorian place we used to go to in London, with old white tiles and freezing cold changing rooms. The pool at Garvick is behind the big hotel, in a modern building that's all pine and glass. "Everyone uses it," I told her. "The primary schools bring their kids for swimming lessons, and there's Aquafizz in the evenings. Mum goes sometimes."

"Cool," Del said.

She looked a bit overawed, though, and when we'd got changed and went into the pool itself, I could see she'd been right when she said she wasn't much of a swimmer. She did a sort of splashy breaststroke with her head up and her eyes tight shut, and she never ventured out of the shallow end. She loved the Jacuzzi, though. "It really floats you!" she said. Every time the bubbles stopped, she pressed the button to start them again. Mum says you need a bit of flesh on your bones to float easily. I don't have any trouble that way, but skinny people like Del tend to sink. She was quite happy, though, pottering about between the whirlpool and the warm splash where you can sit in the shallow water and let the jet pour over you, so I tanked up and down for a bit, then floated on my back, looking at the rippling reflections of the water on the pale wood ceiling. I looked across at Del from time to time, and saw her go into the sauna that's supposed to be for club members only, then back into the changing room, then out again to the Jacuzzi. She seemed fine. That's one thing to be said for a swimming pool, I thought – it's good and safe. The only thing you could possibly do is drown, and with pool attendants standing around, even that's not likely.

After a bit, I needed to go to the loo – swimming always makes me feel like that – so I climbed out and went into the changing room. Del was standing under the hot shower, with her face turned up to the cascade of water.

"You okay?" I asked.

"Yeah, fine."

On the back of the toilet door, there was a scrawl of red felt-tip. An upright line with a half-open circle round it. I had such a rush of rage that I felt hot all over. I'd been in the same cubicle before I went in the pool, and the mark hadn't been there then. There was no doubt about it now – the capital D was for Del. I went marching out and stood in the shower next to her.

"That was you, wasn't it?" I said. "The mark on the door."

"What door?"

"The toilet."

"So?"

"It mucks the place up, Del, it's horrible."

"It's only a wee one."

"I know, but—"

I ran out of words. If she didn't see what I was on about, what was the use? I didn't want to sound like some nagging grown-up. But the morning was spoilt, and I didn't want to stay here any more. What if somebody spotted it and we were thrown out? I padded wetly across to my locker and got out my towel and shampoo, then went back to the showers.

"You want some of this?" I offered. "It gets the chlorine out of your hair."

"Thanks. I never thought to bring my gel, I'm gonnae look terrible." She sounded quite casual.

I washed my hair in murderous silence, then went

77

off and got dressed. By the time I sat down to do my trainers up, the rage had given way to depression. Whatever I tried to do, Del seemed determined to ruin it. I'd thought we were getting on better, but now I felt that things were back at square one.

Del had put her clothes on as well – black shoes, black tights, short skirt, skimpy top – and she was drying her hair under the wall drier. "I never reckoned to get it so wet," she said. "When I've been swimming before, I keep my head out the water."

Actually, I thought her hair looked a lot better. Without the spikes, it hung over her forehead in a dark mass, like a pony, and the beetroot colour had finally gone.

Mum had given us some money for drinks at the Poolside café afterwards, but Del wasn't keen on that idea, so we bought a couple of Cokes and took them out with us.

She wouldn't sit on the bench in the rose garden, either. "Let's go," she said. Maybe she had the same fear as me, that a pool attendant would come raging out and collar us for defacing the property. Maybe she thought I'd tell on her.

She needn't have worried. Even though I didn't like it, I'd never have let her down. Somewhere in the middle of all this mess was the obstinate, rather hopeless wish that it could be all right and we'd find some sort of friendship. We walked down the drive between the woodlands that are full of snowdrops in spring, and when we were out of sight of the hotel, Del sat down on the low wall where the fields start, and opened her can of Coke. She drank half of it, then asked, "What we goin' to do, then?"

"Find somewhere to eat our picnic." I was ravenous after swimming, I always am – and the Coke sloshing around in my empty stomach only made me hungrier.

"Then what?"

"I don't know." I didn't care much. What was the use? With an effort, I asked, "What would you like to do?"

Del shrugged. With her shaggy, newly washed hair and no mascara, she looked much younger, and I felt ashamed of my bad temper. After all, she didn't know this place. She had no idea where things were or what could be done. It wasn't fair to ask her to choose. But then, what would she like? Half-heartedly, I said, "Crazy Golf?"

"No, thanks." She drank some more Coke, then added, "Go ahead if you want, though."

"Not me, I'd feel a prat."

Well, then, why did you suggest it? She didn't actually

say the words, but they hung in the air between us. Del looked round her and sighed. Then she looked again. "Hey, could we go up there?"

She pointed across at the blue silhouette of the Devil's Leap, away behind the trees. It's the highest of Broray's hills – a mountain, really. I didn't know what to say. I'd only been up there once, with Mum and Dad, and there'd been a big fuss about taking waterproofs and sweaters and telling the Baileys we were going. Dad even had a map and a compass – you'd have thought we were tackling the north face of the Eiger. And in fact it hadn't been all that steep. It was a long haul up to the top, right enough, and I'd got quite out of breath, but it wasn't a hands-and-feet clamber like I'd expected.

I looked at my watch. Just gone half-past one. We had the whole afternoon.

"Doesnae matter if you don't fancy it," Del said, because I hadn't answered.

"It's farther than it looks," I told her. "And it's quite rocky at the top."

"So?"

"Have you got anything with you to put on? Just in case the weather changes." A small cloud was hanging over the blue peak.

"Aye. In my bag."

"I've got my denim jacket."

"We going, then?"

"I suppose we could." I was trying hard to be sensible. Del's clumpy shoes were probably all right for walking – the heels weren't high.

"What you worried about?" Del asked.

I didn't want to seem like a wimp, but on the other hand – "It's just that people go up there in summer clothes and sandals, and if they get caught in bad weather and can't find their way down, the Mountain Rescue has to turn out, and a helicopter from the mainland sometimes – I mean, people have died up there."

"Okay," said Del. "It was just an idea."

That's what did it, really, the way she gave up without any protest, as if she was used to nice things never actually happening. So I said, "Come on – we'll go for it." After all, there was no need to go all the way to the top. If we got tired or the weather turned funny, we could always come back. We'd be sensible.

Ten

It took us half an hour or so to get to the track that leads up the first stage of the Devil's Leap, and when it got steeper, Del slowed down a bit, to my relief. By now I was absolutely ravenous.

We'd left the fields behind, and were out on the open moor, and I sat down in the heather and said firmly, "Lunchtime."

For once, Del was hungry, too. "I could murder a sandwich," she said.

We ate everything, including the by-now melting chocolate wafers and the apples, and I stuffed the wrappings back into my rucksack. Then we went on up.

Above us, the wisp of cloud seemed larger. Nothing to worry about, I told myself. We were closer to it, that was all, so it naturally looked bigger. I didn't say anything. I'd settled into that steady state you get into on a hill, when your breathing sort of fits with your steps. You need more breath for talking, and it upsets everything.

"We must be near the top," Del said cheerfully. "That wee cloud is quite close now."

I didn't answer. When we'd gone a bit farther, mistiness started to obscure the sun. The visibility was fine, though – it was only like a normal, cloudy day. Del was ahead of me, still going like a train. For someone so skinny, she was surprisingly strong.

The cloud thickened, and dampness started to blow in the wind. I stopped, and said, "Del, I think we ought to go back."

She looked down at me from farther up the path, and said, "Why?"

"If it gets worse, we won't be able to see."

For once, Del argued. "Ah, c'mon. We must be almost at the top by now."

She was probably right. We'd got to the steep bit. Another few minutes, and we'd probably be there. And I could see her point. Who'd want to say they'd *almost* climbed the Devil's Leap?

So we kept going. It took us a good ten minutes, getting up the last rocky bit, but then we were at the summit. There's a glassed-in panorama thing up there, showing all the peaks you can see – or at least, could do if it was clear. But by now the dampness had thickened, and there was nothing out there but shifting white mist. Del didn't seem to mind. "At least I can tell Sylvie I've been in a cloud," she said.

I hauled my denim jacket out of my rucksack and put it on. I'd been too hot on the way up to want it, but now the wet chilliness was starting to get to me. Del undid the string of her Mickey Mouse bag, and pulled out a cotton cardigan-thing, pink and hopelessly skimpy. I started to say, "Is that all you've got—" but a can of some kind fell out with it and bounced away down the rocks.

"Oh, rats," Del said. And she dropped the skimpy top and went off after it.

"Del, don't!" I shouted. "It's steep down there!"

She didn't answer.

"Del, come back! Don't be so stupid, just leave it." I didn't know what she'd dropped, but whatever it was, nothing is worth risking your life for.

" 'S all right." Her voice sounded horribly distant.

I panicked. "For God's sake, Del, *come back*!"

Then I heard her fall. A rattle of stones, a slide, a sickening thud. I heard myself screaming her name, but into silence. I was sobbing as I grabbed up both rucksacks, rammed the stupid pink top into hers, pushed that into mine, shoved my arms through the straps. I started out down the rocks. My knees had gone as weak as jelly. Breathlessly, I kept shouting.

At last she answered, from somewhere not far below me. "Fran?" She sounded very shaky.

"I'm coming, hang on. Keep talking, I can't see you."

"I'm here. There's a big rock."

I saw the shape of it in the mist, then I could see Del. She was hunched beside the rock, cradling her left hand.

"What have you done?"

"I'm okay. Just my wrist."

I climbed down the last few metres and crouched beside her. There was a ragged hole in the knee of her tights and blood oozed from a messy gash, but that wasn't the worst thing. She released her wrist a little and showed me, and my heart turned over. The hand was already blue and swollen, and the whole thing looked wrong, somehow.

"I think it's broken," Del said. "It's awfu' sore." Then she looked at me and added, "Sorry, Fran."

"Don't worry." She was shivering, so I took off my jacket and put it round her shoulders. I was thinking furiously. We'd have to get back up the hill to find the path. If we tried to work our way down from here, we'd be bound to get lost, and there was no knowing how steep it was. But Del couldn't climb while she was hugging her wrist – you needed at least one good hand to grab at things with. I said, "We'll have to make a sling or something."

Del nodded. Her teeth were chattering.

There was nothing to use except the damp swimsuits and towels. I hauled mine out of the rucksack and unrolled them. Wrapping the swimmie round her wrist was a bit frightening – I kept imagining the torn muscles and broken bones in there, and hated the idea that I was hurting her. Del gave a quick gasp once, but she didn't make any fuss.

I held up the towel, trying to work out the best way to use it, and Del said, "Best tie it right round me if you can." So that's what I did, knotting it behind her neck and further down her back, with the injured wrist held close against her. Then she struggled to her feet. She tried to make me take my jacket back, but I wasn't having that. I put it round her shoulders again and zipped it up as far as it would go, then put her skimpy pink cardigan on myself, for what it was worth.

As I stooped to tie the string of my rucksack, I caught sight of the thing Del had dropped, just a glimpse of metal from under a clump of whin. When

I picked it up, I saw that it was a spray can. Royal Blue. I didn't say anything, just stuffed it in my rucksack and hitched my arms through the straps, but Del met my eyes. She made a face that wasn't a smile. "Your parents are going to go ballistic this time," she said.

It took a long time to get down. The cloud had enveloped the hill, and the drifting rain brought its wetness close to the skin, penetrating easily through our useless clothes. My trainers slipped on the wet stones, and I slithered and fell a couple of times, though I only bruised my bum. Del's clumpy shoes had a better grip, luckily, but she had a terrible time of it coming down the steep part of the hill. Shifting from rock to rock jarred her wrist, and her knee was bleeding. I heard her grunt with pain once or twice, but she wouldn't take my hand – she said she'd be better on her own.

I was heading for the swimming-pool hotel, because that was the first place we'd come to and I could phone Mum from there, but as we turned into the drive, a car was coming towards us, and it stopped. A woman wound the window down and said, "Are you all right?"

We weren't, of course. Both of us were soaking

wet, and Del looked so white and awful, I thought she was going to pass out at any moment.

I explained what had happened, and the woman said, "Oh, my goodness. Get in, both of you. We're going straight to the hospital." She turned out to be Mrs Head, Kirsty's mother, from the south end. She works as a receptionist at the hotel, and she was just going off duty. Kirsty is friends with Julie, so I knew the whole story would be round the school in no time. That was all I needed. Now I'd be known as the prat who took someone up the Devil's Leap and nearly got her killed. Oh, well – nothing I could do about that. It didn't matter much, anyway. The important thing was Del.

Our hospital is tiny, just a couple of wards and half a dozen nurses, but it copes with more or less everything. Del was hoping she'd get to go in a helicopter to the big hospital on the mainland, but the nurse who took charge of us was quite unfazed, as if this sort of thing happened all the time – which I suppose it does.

"What a couple of drowned rats," she said cheerfully. She wrapped us both in red blankets, and left me sitting in the waiting area while she took Del off to be X-rayed.

Mrs Head asked if there was anything else she

could do, but there wasn't really. So she got me a cup of coffee out of the machine and wouldn't take the money for it, then went off home. And I phoned Mum.

Del was right – ballistic was the word.

"You went *where*? With no proper clothing and no map? Fran, are you out of your *mind*?"

There was quite a lot more. I should have told someone, I should have phoned home, I should never have gone today at all, not without climbing boots and macs and someone responsible with us. Then she said we were to stay right there and *not move* (as if there was any choice about it.) She'd be over straight away.

They all came, Mum and Dad and Barney, who was really upset. He kept wandering off because he knew something had happened to Del and he wanted to find her. One of us brought him back each time, and he started to get cross about it.

"She'll be here in a minute," I told him. "You don't have to worry, she's all right, honestly."

It wasn't really Barney I was talking to. Mum was frantic because the nurse had been in and told us the X-ray had shown a nasty break, and they were going to give Del "just a wee whiff" of anaesthetic while they set her wrist. That was quite some time ago, and we were still waiting.

"It's a nightmare," Mum said. "She might have died. Just imagine having to phone Mrs Mountford—" She shook her head and clamped a hanky to her nose. There were tears in her eyes.

Dad put his hand over hers and said, "It's all right, love. She'll be fine." But he was looking a bit grim, and I knew he wasn't happy with what I had told him. The trouble was, I didn't want to say anything about the spray can. The business about the Talky Bear was bad enough without dragging in a whole new thing about graffiti.

After another few minutes, Dad asked the question I'd dreaded. "I still don't see what happened, Fran. You were standing at the summit – and then what? She can't have taken a nose-dive for no reason. Were you mucking about, or what?"

"She – dropped something. And she went to get it, only she slipped." I risked a quick glance at him, knowing my face was scarlet. Please don't ask what it was she dropped, I prayed. Please. And he didn't.

I knew that wasn't the last of it, but Mum calmed down a bit, and Barney perched on a chair instead of barging about. Dad gave him his Game Boy, which he'd refused earlier, and although he grumbled a bit, he started pressing the buttons, and within a few minutes he was absorbed in some dreadful Japanese sword-fight. That's the great thing about Barney, he can get off into his own world so easily once he starts to pay attention to it. I don't have a different world to escape to – I'm always stuck with this one. Letting my mind wander is even worse, because then I start imagining disasters, like Mum does.

Sitting there, it was a struggle not to picture a doctor entering, grave-faced. "We did everything we could . . . I'm so sorry . . ." What other explanation could there be for this long wait? Something must have gone wrong.

Mum looked at me – and suddenly she was the one doing the comforting. "Don't worry," she said. "Sorry, Fran – you've had a bad time, too."

I was beginning to feel really shaky. But somehow, when you absolutely can't bear things any more, something else always seems to happen – and at that moment, the nurse came back with Del. Mum grabbed Barney to stop him from rushing to hug her, and we all stood up, me still clutching the red blanket. Del's arm was in a sling and her face was chalk-white, but her wrist wasn't in a plaster cast as I'd expected. Her hand was heavily bandaged over a wide splint that ran from underneath her fingers to her arm.

"Now, she'll need to come in tomorrow for a proper plaster," the nurse said. "It's too swollen just now, but by the morning it should have gone down. We'll X-ray it again, make sure everything's in the right place. Can you be here by eleven?"

"No problem," said Dad. "How're you feeling, Del?"

"Okay," Del said. She looked awful, even worse than when she'd come off the boat on that first morning. Sort of – fragile. With her floppy thatch of hair and my jacket slung round her shoulders, and a white dressing on her knee, she was like a little kid who's fallen down. Not the old Del at all. And I, in Del's skimpy cardigan and an untidy blanket, wasn't the old Fran.

"One bathing costume and one towel," the nurse said briskly, handing Mum a plastic bag. "That was a very sensible bit of first aid your daughter did – you should be proud of her."

Nobody seemed much impressed by this Brownie point. Barney was moaning in concern over Del's bandaged hand, stroking it with one finger, and Mum and Dad were in a general flap about distributing warm clothes and getting us out to the car.

"She can have a couple of paracetemol if it's a bit uncomfortable tonight," said the nurse, "and we'll see you in the morning, right?"

"Right," said Dad.

Mum didn't say anything. It was all too much.

Eleven

Sun was shining through the curtains when I woke the next morning, although it was still early. I ached a bit from falling yesterday on that dreadful return down the hill.

I'd gone to sleep in the car on the way home. I don't know if Del slept as well, but when we got in, she didn't want anything to eat and Mum put her straight to bed with two hot-water bottles and a mug of cocoa. I was ravenous, of course, well ready for hotpot and baked potatoes.

Dad phoned the Holiday woman, Mrs Mountford. It sounded from our end of it as if she was giving him a bad time.

"No, there wasn't anyone with them. We didn't actually know they were ... yes, I'm aware that she's our responsibility, but ... no, of course not." He was managing to keep his temper, but he looked pretty exasperated. "Yes, we'll let you know. I'll phone you tomorrow. 'Bye."

Mum asked, "Shot at dawn?"

"Hanged, drawn and quartered," said Dad. "She wants me to ring her with an update when we've been to the hospital."

"Thanks for tackling her, love," Mum said. "I just couldn't.

"Any time," said Dad stoically. And I went upstairs for a hot bath and bed.

Thinking about it this morning, with Del's cocoa mug still half-full on the bedside table, I felt really sorry for Mum. The whole thing had been her idea, and she was probably wishing now that she'd never thought of it.

Del herself was still fast asleep. All I could see of her was a tuft of dark hair and the fingertips that stuck out from the bandaged hand on the pillow beside her face. The spray can stood on the chest of drawers at the end of her bed. I'd put it there last night, when I emptied the things out of my bag. No point in hiding it, I'd thought. She'd risked her life for the wretched thing, so we could hardly pretend it didn't exist.

What a weird thing to do, anyway. Would I have

gone down those rocks in the mist just to retrieve a spray can? I couldn't imagine it being that important. It must have meant a lot to Del, though. Maybe they were quite expensive. I got out of bed and went over to the chest of drawers to have a look.

The label on the can said three pounds, thirty-seven – and it was printed with the name of the hardware shop in Garvick, *Indoors And Out*. Three thirty-seven was quite a lot, right enough. Suddenly, I was wondering if Del had paid for it. Could this be another thing like the Talky Bear?

Leaving the spray can in view didn't seem such a good idea, after all. I felt a bit grubby, even handling it. I pulled her Mickey Mouse rucksack open and shoved the can inside – and at that moment, Del rolled over in bed and looked at me, the back of her good hand above her eyes as if the morning daylight was too much.

"Hi," I said. My face was flaming, of course. "Just putting your things back. Are you feeling better?"

"Mmm."

I got back into bed and asked, "How's your wrist?"

"Okay." After a pause, she added, "My knee's sore, though."

"I bet."

There was a much longer silence, then Del said, "Listen, thanks for yesterday."

I didn't know what to say. The whole thing had been my fault. If I'd been a bit firmer, we'd have turned back, and she'd never have fallen. But she wouldn't have thanked me for that.

Mum tapped on the door at just that moment, then opened it and came in with a laden tray.

"Breakfast in bed," she said. "I thought you needed a bit of cossetting." She slid the tray onto the bedside table between us and picked up the cold cocoa mug from last night. "Remember we've to be at the hospital by eleven," she added.

I reached up and hugged her. "You're brilliant," I said.

Del didn't say anything – she seemed astonished. Mum gave me a kiss, then bent down and gave Del one too. "How's your wrist?" she asked.

"Fine," said Del.

When the door had closed, she said, "Your mum's so nice."

At least, that's what she meant to say, but on the last word, something went wrong with her voice, and I saw that she was struggling with tears.

I got out of bed and knelt beside her, and she put her good hand over mine and gripped it tightly.

"See, my mum," she said unsteadily, "she got leukaemia."

"I know. At least, I didn't know what it was, but they told me she . . ." My voice tailed away. This was something I hadn't got my head round, not properly. It's easy to think, "Oh, how awful", the way you do when you see starving children on the telly, but it's not happening to you or anyone you know, and that makes it different. But this was real.

Del let go of my hand, and smoothed the duvet carefully. Somehow, she was managing to keep everything under control. "They said she shouldnae have the baby," she said. "Only Mum wanted it, she said it would be great for me to have a wee brother or sister, it would be someone to grow up with. I remember her saying that." After a pause, she went on, "Dad says if she hadnae had Sylvie she'd ha' been all right, but I don't know. He goes on about it, specially if he's bevvied. My gran says I've no' to blame him, it's just he never got over my mum dyin'. But, see—" There was another hard pause. "He doesnae like Sylvie."

"Perhaps he does, really." Why was I making excuses for this man who sounded so horrible? Maybe I couldn't bear to believe it. "He could be just – not wanting to seem soft, or something."

Del shook her head. "She puts him in mind of Mum," she said bleakly. "Sylvie's fair, see, like Mum was. Him and me, we're both dark. Only I change mine. I'm thinkin' to try highlights." Then she looked at the laden tray with its yoghurt and cereals and cheese and fruit and you-name-it, and managed a grin. "You goin' to peel me a grape, then?"

"You'll be lucky," I said – but the way I felt at that moment, if I'd thought she really meant it, I'd have done it.

There was another long wait at the hospital, because they were dealing with an emergency. A young man was wheeled in from the ambulance, his head swathed in bandages and a dribble of blood coming from his mouth. There was a drip bottle on the trolley, with a tube disappearing under the blanket.

Del was fascinated. "What d'you suppose he's done?" she asked Mum.

"Goodness knows. Car accident, perhaps."

One of the ambulancemen heard her, and said, "He slipped on the rocks, out fishing. Gave himself a nasty smack on the head."

"Oh." Del wasn't satisfied with that, though, and when the trolley and its burden had been moved on, she and Mum started discussing the possible causes of the blood coming from the young man's mouth. Had he bitten his tongue? Knocked a tooth out? Or was it something really serious, like broken ribs and a punctured lung?

I didn't much want to listen. Not that I'm squeamish – I'm quite interested in looking at dead birds and that sort of thing – but humans are too close for comfort. It's as if their injuries are mine, and I can't think about them without a nasty twinge.

"Jim was saying you'd like to be a doctor," Mum said to Del. "That's what I wanted to do when I was a kid."

I said, "*Did* you?"

"Oh, yes. But there were three of us, and my dad didn't earn much, and I was the eldest – well, you know all that. So I was desperate to earn some money and help out a bit. Medicine's such a long training, and it's years before you get paid anything. And it's hellish hard work."

"I wouldnae mind the work," Del said.

"Neither would I," Mum agreed. "I suppose I'm just making excuses. Looking back, I wish I'd gone for it. We'd have coped somehow, and we'd have been much better off in the end. And I'd have some qualifications. So don't make the same mistake, Del. Grab the chance now, while you've got it."

"What chance?" said Del gloomily. "My dad would have a fit."

"He'd get used to it. He'd end up really proud of you."

Del shook her head. "You don't know him."

I seemed to be completely outside this conversation. Mum and Del sounded like two women in a launderette, talking about families and money with shared experience in common – and I didn't even know my mother had wanted to be a doctor. I'd always assumed that taking charge of the Post Office was quite a big, important thing for her to do.

"Now, look," Mum was saying to Del, "you're going to have to tackle this, sooner or later. I'm not saying anything against your dad – I'm sure he has his reasons for being the way he is. My mum had her reasons, too, and they were good ones, but all the same, I ended up being so sorry for her that I was in a sort of cage. I couldn't do what I wanted to do, because it seemed too selfish."

"It's no' just that," said Del. "See, there's Sylvie."

"And she's what – six?"

"Aye. Seven in October."

Mum nodded and said, "That's a tough one. I can see she relies on you a lot. But your school work matters as well. You need to be getting down to it now if you're thinking of medical school. Isn't there any way you can get some help? Couldn't the Social Services—"

"*No!*" Del looked terrified. "You won't say anything to them, will you? If they think we cannae cope wi' Sylvie, she'll get put in care. There's lots of folk had their weans taken away. The woman upstairs did."

"Don't panic," Mum said. "I wouldn't dream of saying anything – it's not my business. But, Del, by the time you're in the sixth year, Sylvie won't be so young. She'll be into secondary school herself. And you wouldn't have to leave home or anything – you could study in Glasgow."

"Maybe." Del sounded doubtful.

A nurse came in and said, "Right, my dear, we're ready for you now. Sorry you've had to wait."

Del stood up. As she went off with the nurse, she glanced over her shoulder and said, "Great idea, though." And grinned.

Twelve

After yet another longish wait, Del came back with her wrist in a plaster cast that covered her whole hand and just left her thumb and her fingers sticking out. She said the X-rays had been really interesting.

Mum took us straight home, because we'd been ages, and Mrs McKinnon would be wanting to get away for her lunch. It had turned into a hot day, and the kitchen was stifling because we keep the Rayburn on, otherwise it's chilly at nights – and anyway, we use it for cooking. The cats were sprawled on their favourite chair, and Del edged herself between them.

"You mind your claws," she told Danny, who reached a sleepy paw across her bare leg. She hadn't put tights on this morning, perhaps because her knee was sore. They'd put a fresh dressing on it at the hospital.

After lunch, she and I did the washing up – except that Del found she couldn't hold anything in her left hand, because her thumb and her fingers wouldn't meet across the plaster. "What a bummer," she said, gazing at it in dismay.

"Good excuse to get out of the housework," I said. Stupid remark. Del gave me a look that said clearly that if *she* didn't do the housework, nobody did. For a dizzying moment, I thought of what it would be like here without Mum. Could I do the shopping and cooking and look after Dad and Barney and make packed lunches and bring people breakfast in bed? No way. Suddenly I wanted to go into the shop and see that everyone was there, safe and normal. I pushed open the door, and Del disentangled herself from the cat and came too.

Dad was checking out Mrs Robertson's groceries, and Mum was in the Post Office, putting stamps on a parcel for old Mr Yates, who has a daughter in Australia. Barney was stacking tins of soup on the shelf, very carefully, the way he does everything. Mrs Pringle came in, and he beamed at her and asked, in his way, if he could go and pat her dog. Trixie is a West Highland terrier, one of those little white things, and he thinks she's lovely. So off he went to where Trixie was hitched to the hook outside. Dad put the hook up after Davey Barr's Alsatian piddled on someone's leg. We used to allow dogs in the shop, but that was the end.

Mum came out from behind the counter when Mr Yates had gone shuffling off, and said, "Why don't you two go down on the beach? A bit of sunshine would do you good. Just take it easy, Del – I expect you're still feeling shattered. Perhaps Barney would like to go with you."

Barney at that moment came in, and started a complicated business of suggesting to Mrs Pringle that he could carry her shopping home for her and hold Trixie's lead, and Mrs Pringle was quite keen on that idea. So Del and I went on our own.

It was the first time I'd ever walked over that familiar grass across the road with anyone else, apart from my family. I'd so often thought how great it would be to have a friend with me, someone I could take to my favourite sheltered spots where you can sit with your back against the rock and watch the gannets diving into the sea. And now at last it was happening. Here was Del, walking a bit stiffly and perhaps not into gannets, but – I hardly dared think this – a friend.

And she did like the gannets. "What's all those

white splashes in the sea?" she asked. I explained how the birds dived out of the sky for fish, and she watched a couple of them do it and said, "They go in helluva fast."

I went on about how their beaks are kind of reinforced. I'd had a good look at a dead one I found last year. It was amazingly big, and you could see that the head was protected behind the hard bit that extends from the beak itself right up between the eyes.

"I put bread out for the birds at home," Del said. "Down on the drying green. Only half the time the cats eat it. Dogs, too – there's a lot of dogs."

"Whose are they?"

"Dunno. Don't think they have owners."

We were walking down the path that led to the beach, between sprawling brambles and thickets of tall knotweed. The tide was out and there were lagoons of shallow water left on the sand, and when we got down there I slipped my sandals off to paddle. Del tried to stay on the dry bit at first, but before long she bent down to tug at her laces.

"We can leave our shoes over there on a rock," I said. "It saves carrying them."

"You sure they'll be okay?"

" 'Course they will." I took both pairs and went

up the beach to park them on a limpet-encrusted slab that was well clear of the tide, and when I came back, Del was standing ankle-deep in a pool, watching the water wash across her feet. "It's warm!" she said. "Hey, this is brilliant!" And she set off towards the sea, where ripple after white-edged ripple spread across the sand.

You can spend hours on a beach. Del loved it. We dabbled about in the shady water between the rocks, watching small things dart for shelter and touching the waving red tentacles of sea anenomes with a bit of seaweed to see how they folded in on themselves and turned into ruby-coloured lumps of jelly. Del thought the worm-casts that came writhing out of the sand were the actual worms, but she didn't find it at all yukky when I explained that the little coiled heaps were just sand that had been through the body of a rag-worm or lug-worm. She wanted to see one, but we hadn't a spade, and you have to dig like mad to catch them. Dad and I do it sometimes – he's quite keen on fishing. He says if things go well, he'll buy a boat next year, just a small one.

Del went wandering along the edge of the sea, staring down into the water, then she suddenly said, "Hey, what are these?" She bent down and dipped with her good hand, and brought up a blue-black winkle shell, no bigger than a marble. I splashed across to look. The shell didn't have the usual snail-like beastie in it – instead, a lot of busy little legs stuck out, the two biggest ones ending in tiny claws. I was thrilled. "It's a hermit crab! I've only seen pictures of them in books. They don't have shells of their own, so they have to find an empty one to live in. These are just baby ones."

"There's millions," said Del. And she was right. Each shallow layer of water that came rippling in brought a scatter of the little crabs in their winkle shells and cast them up on the sand. As the water sank away, they turned themselves the right way up if need be, and scuttled back into the water, making narrow, raggedy trails as they went. The whole beach was marked with these little tracks and studded with travelling winkle shells. I'd never seen them before, even though I'd been down there dozens of times. It seemed like a special magic of the day.

"What'll they do when they get bigger?" Del asked.

"They'll have to find a bigger shell. Move house."

"Poor wee things. What if they don't find one?"

"They'll get eaten."

"That's terrible."

"Not really. I mean, we eat fish and chips."

"Think I'll be a vegetarian."

Trying to cheer her up, I said, "The picture I saw was of a really big one, in a shell the size of an ice-cream cone."

"Just luck," said Del. She moved her foot in the water, gently touching one of the small travellers with her toe.

"Suppose so."

We didn't say any more. Hermit crabs aren't the only things that depend on luck.

We were there all afternoon, and the tide turned and started to creep back in across the shore. Soon the water was halfway up our legs instead of just to our ankles, and as an extra deep wave came washing in, Del said, "Yikes!" and bent to inspect her knee. The dressing on it was soaked with seawater, but I told her not to worry – the sea is great at healing things. Mum says it's the salt.

I glanced up the beach to make sure our shoes were all right, and saw that the lagoons had joined into wider sheets of water, and the rock with our shoes on it was an island. We paddled and waded our way towards it, rescued the shoes and took them across the dry sand farther up, where the grass starts. Then we sat down to let our feet dry in the sun. I don't suppose Mum thought we'd go paddling, or she'd have given us towels.

Del lay down with her good arm behind her head, cradling the plastered wrist in the other hand, and closed her eyes. She didn't move for a long time, and I wondered if she'd gone to sleep. I didn't mind. It's not often you know you're happy, but at that moment, sitting with my arms round my knees and tasting the saltiness of my skin, I felt that, no matter what happened afterwards, I would remember this for ever. I turned my head sideways, hearing the wash of the sea, and the sun burned red through my closed eyelids.

Del sat up and rubbed some of the drying sand off her feet. Then she said, "Fran—"

"Mmm?"

"See yesterday."

I opened my eyes and looked at her. She was frowning.

"Does your mum know about the spray can?"

"No."

Del did some more sand-brushing. It was my turn to say something. Explain why I'd hidden it from sight in her bag, ask why it had been so important. But I didn't. I closed my eyes again, and pretended

110

that the day was too lovely to bother about such details. And the happiness had gone.

Thirteen

The next morning, there was no breakfast in bed.
That had been a one-off, because of Del's accident.
So I lay there and thought about the minutes slipping
away. This time tomorrow, we'd be driving over the
hill to put Del on the boat. This was the last day.
And it was already late – gone half-past ten.

I looked across at Del's bed, but she was sleeping
as soundly as some furry animal that's curled up for
the winter, and the threadbare rabbit lay on the
floor, unnoticed. I wished I hadn't blown my chance
to talk to her yesterday. There were unspoken things
between us that prevented this from being a proper
friendship, and unless I faced them, she was going
to slip away like a missed catch, when the ball just
brushes your fingers and is gone. Why hadn't I had
a bit more courage?

Dad was better at it than me. Last night, when he

and I had been washing up after tea, he tackled our little patch of difficulty straight out.

"So what's the story, Fran?" he said.

"Story?" I always panic and try to sound innocent, I don't know why.

"Come on. I want to know what happened when you and Del were up the hill. I know there's something you don't want to say, but it's got to be faced."

I hung coffee mugs on their hooks, and wished this moment wasn't happening. The TV was prattling away in the sitting room next door, and I heard Barney laughing.

Dad scooped a bit of uneaten chicken pie from Del's plate into the cats' dish and said, "I won't tell her."

"Promise?"

"Promise."

So I blurted out the whole thing. The graffiti in Garvick and on the changing-room door, the marker that fell out when she was unpacking on the first day – and the spray can. I felt awful, as if I was betraying Del.

Dad seemed quite cheerful. "Thank heaven for that," he said when I'd finished. "I thought you were going to tell me she was doing drugs."

"Dad! Del's not like that!"

He looked at me and said, "How would you know? People who use drugs don't have horns and a tail, you know, they're the same as you and me. Quite a lot of the kids in my school were on one thing or another, and I used to worry about it, but there are no easy answers. If your life is pretty dismal, it's natural enough to grab at a bit of happiness, chemical or not. But once the habit gets hold of you, it's dangerous. So hellishly expensive, all else apart."

"I know." The idea of taking something that would come right into my brain and make things seem different scares me stiff, and I'd never do it. But Dad really had thought that Del might be a drug-user. No wonder he'd wanted to send her home.

As if he'd heard my thoughts, he said, "You can see why I was worried. People don't get hooked because some shifty character comes up and tries to sell them some pill or other. It's always because a friend does it. Someone they admire."

"Suppose so." If Del had said, "Hey, try this, it's dead brilliant," would I have done? I had to admit that it wasn't impossible. If you very much want to be liked, it's amazing what you'll do. That's why I'd gone on up the hill when I knew it was dodgy –

because I wanted to keep in with Del and be with her, whatever she wanted to do.

Dad let the water out of the sink and swished it round with the washing-up brush. "Not that I'm exactly keen on graffiti," he said. "But with any luck, she'll grow out of it." Then he dried his hands and we went into the sitting room to watch the telly with the others.

So here I was on Friday morning, lying in bed with the whole thing going round and round in my mind. I'd come clean with Dad, but not with Del. I just couldn't. If she'd stolen the Talky Bear and perhaps the spray can as well, I didn't want to know.

It still seemed very odd that she'd want a Talky Bear. I couldn't see how anyone could get hooked on a furry toy that's not in the least like a real animal with muscles and bone. Perhaps it was something to do with living in a city, where almost everything you look at has been made by people. Shops, flats, pavements, roads – they've all been built. You can't build an animal or a tree, they're just themselves.

Perhaps Del was lonely, in a way. She didn't seem to be, because she got on so easily with people, much better than I did, but there was no one much she could really talk to about the big things. Her gran and the hairdressing aunt were probably okay, but you have to be careful what you say to grannies and aunts, or they might think you're dropping hints about something you want or something they ought to do. And that's not on, really. Maybe that was why Del seemed so grown up. She didn't ask anyone, just did what she thought she'd do. And if that didn't fit with other people's ideas, tough.

She must think I was a terrible wimp. Not grown up at all.

This was not a pleasant idea, and after a bit, I'd had enough of lying in bed and thinking miserable thoughts, so I got up and collected my clothes quietly, and went off to the bathroom to get dressed, so as not to wake Del.

I went down to the kitchen and got a carton of apple juice out of the fridge. The breakfast things were still on the table, and propped against the teapot was an open letter, as if it was asking to be read. I knew at once what it was. The scholarship result. I hardly wanted to look.

The letter was on thick white paper with a coat of arms at the top. I scanned it so fast that the words seemed to jump. *Braeforth School Scholarship Examination . . . delighted to inform you . . . successful . . . can therefore offer Frances a place at this school, commencing in the coming Autumn Term . . .*

So I'd passed. I could be one of those glossy girls who strolled across lawns with books under their arms. Mum and Dad would be so thrilled. There wasn't any choice, was there, not really. I couldn't let them down.

Somehow, I didn't want to go into the shop for the hugs and congratulations that were waiting. I drank my apple juice and rinsed the glass, looked at the cluttered table and wondered whether to clear it, and decided against. Without really intending to, I found myself going out of the door and heading across the road to the grass and the sea.

I climbed down to my favourite place and sat there. Del wouldn't have made it, with her sore knee and everything. The wall of rock at my back was already warm in the morning sun, and the tough little clumps of thrift were holding up their mauve heads over their rosettes of spiny leaves. Last year I found one that had been torn out of the ground when they were bulldozing a new slipway for dinghies, and its root was about half a metre long. I suppose that's why they can grow in these tiny slits between bare rock. I'd miss them at Braeforth.

I had this tight, unhappy feeling in my tummy, made worse because I didn't want to admit it. The whole situation was deeply embarrassing, because when I thought about Broray High now, it didn't seem so awful. I wasn't exactly looking forward to next term, but Ross had been so nice about the Talky Bear business that he seemed quite human. And outside the Pier shop on that awful morning, the others had said, "Hey, Fran, come back . . ." And now I was never going to find out if they might have turned out to be quite friendly.

Either way, I was going to look like the total spoilt brat – the kid who couldn't hack Broray High and went off to a posh girls' school, or the picker-and-chooser who turned down the chance that had cost her parents so much time and effort. Not a good scene, however you looked at it.

There are times when thinking about a thing only seems to make it worse, and this was one of them. Mum and Dad were in the shop, coping with the Friday morning customers – it was always a busy day – and probably doing a bit of modest boasting about my success, and I couldn't go on skulking out here. So I climbed back up the rocks and crossed the road.

Ross was coming out of our shop door, nose deep in the computer magazine he gets each week, and because he'd been in my thoughts, I felt my face go pink.

"Oh, hi," he said when we'd nearly collided. "How're you doing?"

"Okay."

"How's Del? Still here?"

"She goes tomorrow. Yes, she's all right. Having a late lie-in."

"As visitors do," Ross agreed. He's such a smoothie. Then he said, "Listen, I was really sorry to hear about the accident. Must have been quite hairy, getting her down the hill." He's in the Junior Mountain Rescue, so he's a bit keen on all that.

"We shouldn't have been up there," I said, and he shrugged.

"Difficult with visitors. They always want to see it, do it, buy the T-shirt. And it looked a perfectly good day. Hey, Julie was saying, why don't you come swimming with us?"

"That would be great." Any other time, I'd have been thrilled to bits, but now, I only had half my mind on it.

"We're going on Tuesday. See you on the ten o'clock bus?"

"Yes, sure. Thanks."

"See you, then."

"See you." And, for something to say, I added, "Enjoy your magazine."

Ross had started towards his house, but he turned and said, "You never miss a chance, do you?" He looked offended, and my blush deepened.

"What do you mean?"

"You're always knocking computers. And you don't even know anything about them."

"I don't want to know."

"Well, all right, but you don't have to be so superior about it."

"*Superior*?" I was astounded.

"What else?" said Ross. "You sit on the bus and never say anything – anyone would think I had porridge for brains."

"But it's *you* who doesn't say anything! You just go in and talk to your computer." I was too upset to be tongue-tied. "You're not interested in anything else."

"How would you know?"

For a moment, we glared at each other, then Ross laughed. "Tell you what," he said. "Why don't you come round, and I'll show you what computers can do. Honest, you'll be fascinated."

"But we did some at school and—"

"Like Del says, there's never enough time at school," Ross said firmly. "You just haven't seen it yet, that's all. It's like anything else – riding a bike, learning to swim. Once you suddenly get it, you're there, and it's great."

I wasn't convinced. "I'll take your word for it," I said.

"Sunday, then," said Ross. "After lunch. Okay?"

"Okay."

And off he went into his house. If anyone had told me a week ago that I'd be spending a Sunday afternoon with the oh-so-smooth Ross Bailey, I'd have been gobsmacked.

There were hugs and congratulations when I went into the shop, just as I'd expected. Barney was burbling with excitement because he knew I'd done something special. He didn't understand what it was, but that never bothers him. Del came in a few minutes later, so she got told about it as well.

"Cool," she said.

There were people in the shop while this was happening, and Mum and Dad were both busy, so they didn't notice the glance Del gave me. *If that's what you want.*

Mrs Primrose put her wire basket on the counter and beamed at me. "I hear you've been a clever girl," she said. Mrs P. always sounds very refined – you can see she's the sort who would like the idea of

Braeforth. I wondered how many other people Mum had told.

Over lunch – tinned tomato soup, and shepherd's pie from the freezer – Mum said, "What are you going to do this afternoon? It's your last day, you don't want to waste it."

Del said, "Don't mind." I said we could go down on the beach again, rather hoping for a re-run of yesterday, only this time I'd do it better and not duck out of talking. But Mum had different ideas.

"Why don't you go up to the standing stones? It's a bit of a walk, though – are you up to it, Del?"

"Yeah, fine," said Del.

Barney latched on at once, and started bouncing up and down. "Stones! Stones!" He loves it up there. We were having tinned fruit for afters, and a cherry went flying. Mum put it back on his plate, and he shovelled it in with everything else, then pushed his chair back and stood up. "Come on!" he said.

"Go and get your wellies," Mum told him. "It'll still be wet up there after all the rain we've had."

To be honest, I was sunk in gloom at the thought of having to take Barney. This was my last afternoon with Del, and I hadn't reckoned to spend it Barney-minding.

Mum looked at me and said, "He does love it, Fran."

"Yes, I know."

Del said, "He's no bother."

"No, he won't be any trouble there, he's always quite happy. Don't let him wander off, though – keep an eye on him."

"Sure," said Del, and I felt a bit guilty and said, " 'Course we will."

Dad glanced at his watch and said, "I'll run you along to where the track starts, if you like. That'll save you half an hour or so."

"That'll be great," I said.

Mum said, "If you're not back by six, we'll send out a search party." It was meant as a joke, but it fell a bit flat. Dad just raised his eyebrows, and I almost wished I hadn't told him so much last night. Although he'd been so nice about it, he probably couldn't wait to put Del on the boat and be done with the whole thing.

Fourteen

When we got out of the car, Del said, "Thanks very much." She'd obviously sussed that she wasn't exactly flavour of the month with Dad, and was trying to be extra polite. He said, "No bother," and gave us a wave as he drove off.

We unlatched the gate and went into the field where the track starts. It slopes gently uphill, and there are sheep in there, so Barney closed the gate carefully and put the iron loop over. He likes doing important things, he's always very serious about them. Then he went charging off up the track with his arms flailing like an untidy aeroplane.

"He's great, isn't he," said Del.

I was a bit surprised. Lots of people are kind to Barney, and almost everyone is sorry for him, but there aren't many who really like him.

"He just gets on wi' things," Del explained. "He's

no' always looking for something else, he's ready to be happy whenever he gets the chance."

She was right. Barney gets furious if you interrupt him when he's doing something he's engrossed in, but he never makes himself miserable about wanting things he hasn't got. "Most people don't see that," I said.

"Most people are daft," said Del.

We crossed a couple more fields. Sheep trotted away without much hurry, the half-grown lambs following their mothers, and Barney found muddy tractor ruts and tramped through them. Mum had been right about the wellies.

When we'd passed the farmhouse and byres, we came to the first standing stones. They're just small ones, less than waist high, arranged in a circle that would fit quite easily into Carrach Village Hall. There's a fence round them to keep the sheep out, but it doesn't deter the rabbits, so the grass between the stones is nibbled very short, and it's a wonderfully bright green because of all the droppings.

Barney opened the little gate and went in, and started walking carefully round the stones, touching each one and saying something to it.

"What's he doing?" asked Del.

"I don't know," I said. "He always does that."

Del followed Barney, touching each stone as well, though I don't think she spoke to them. When Barney got back to where he started, he sat down with his back against one of the stones, hugging his knees, and beamed up at Del as she joined him. I sat down as well, and the three of us seemed to be inside a house. Even though it had no walls and no roof, there was something cosy about it.

"What was this place, anyway?" asked Del.

"They call it a hut circle. People would have lived here."

"Bit draughty."

"Don't be daft, it had a roof. Made of big slabs of stone, held up on props. I've seen pictures of it, or some other place like it. The stones are probably underneath where we're sitting, buried under the grass."

"I couldnae fancy bein' stuck out here, miles from anywhere," Del said. "Dead lonely."

"But there wasn't anywhere to be miles *from*," I pointed out. "There weren't any cities – this was it."

"Just one house?"

"There were others, lots of them. And it wouldn't be just one family living in a house like this – there'd be a whole heap of people."

"People," said Barney. He leaned forward and ran his stubby fingers over the short grass, crooning to himself. It sent the shivers down my back a bit, but Del seemed interested. "Are there people here, Barney?" she asked. "Can you see them?"

Barney clapped his hands and laughed, then turned to press his face against the stone he was leaning against. "People," he said.

I wondered if the computers Ross found so exciting would ever be able to explain whatever it was that Barney saw, or felt, or whatever you could call it. Would we one day make a real connection between this time and all others, in the same way that aeroplanes connected us to remote places? A dizzying idea was hovering there somewhere, about the past existing in just the same way as the present moment – and perhaps the future, too. After all, the space between us and the farthest stars existed, even though it was so vast that it melted away into impossibility. For a few moments, the idea was clear and almost simple, then it faded like a rainbow and was gone.

Del got to her feet and ran her hand over the back of her short skirt. "This grass is awfu' damp," she said. "Is there any more of these stones, or is this it?"

"Oh, there's more," I said. "We haven't come to the big ones yet."

"Right. You going to show me the way, Barney?"

"Yeah."

He scrambled to his feet and made for the gate. Usually it took a lot of persuading before we could get him out of the "stone house", as we always called it, but he loved the idea of knowing something that Del didn't. He went rushing off up the track ahead of us, but he turned round from time to time to make sure we were following.

It's quite a long way to the other stones, up the slope to the open moor then down again, past the ruined farm buildings that lie in a hollow on your left, and over three stiles. When we came to the first one, Del looked a bit doubtful, but Barney helped her, and he's very strong and steady about things like that. "It's my knee," she said. "Awfu' sore to bend." The plastered hand didn't help, either, but she seemed okay about that.

You can't see the stones until you're over the last stile. But when you come over the brow of the little hill, there they are, in the broad, open place where three glens meet and there's a glimpse of the open sea, great, craggy things as weathered as old men but twice the height of any human being. Barney went charging towards the nearest one, and flattened himself against it, staring up and laughing.

"What's he up to now?" Del asked.

"He's sky-watching," I said. We'd always called it that. "Haven't you ever done it? You feel as if the whole world is falling sideways, it's great. Come over here, we can try it on this one."

My favourite stone is the one with a slanting shoulder that makes it look as if it's leaning into the wind, and when we got to it, Del stood beside me and said, "What d'you do, then?"

"Just stand close and look up." I put my hands on the cold, rough surface. Above me, the stone towered into the sky, and the small, white clouds that moved along up there triggered the magic. It's a bit like being in a train when another one slowly passes you, and you feel as if you're going backwards. For some reason, the clouds seem to be still, and it's the stone that's moving, in a sideways fall that goes on and on.

"Hey, that's weird," Del said.

I can't keep doing it for too long, otherwise I get dizzy. I looked at Del, who was busy sky-watching, then she looked at me and grinned. "You're a nutter, you know that?" she said. And I grinned back.

The stone we were leaning against was pitted with the marks where people had been carving their initials on it. Some of them must have been hundreds of years old, half-obliterated with moss and the erosion of wind and rain, but there were more recent ones as well, scratched or written. Del put her fingertip on one of them, and said, "It's no' just me."

It was like the moment in the kitchen with Dad.

"Roman soldiers used to carve their names," I said.

"I know," said Del. "We did it in history." But that wasn't what she meant, and we both knew it.

There was an awful pause, then I said, "Why d'you do it?"

"History?"

"No, idiot. Graffiti."

She shrugged. "It's a laugh." But she was watching me carefully. She already knew I didn't like it – I'd said so in the swimming pool.

"What sort of laugh?"

"All these folk. They walk along the street, get on buses an' that, go to their work, drive their cars. They all see what's on the wall, and there's not one of them knows who did it."

"Yes, but—"

"Well, that's it, isn't it? That's what gives you the kick." Del paused for a moment, then went on, "See those really big ones, on the sides of bridges, dangerous places like that, it must be really great. Every time you looked at it, you'd think, *Yeah, that was me.* Brilliant."

I saw what she meant. "Like – making your mark."

"Aye, sort of."

Hundreds of people had stood where we were now. Some of them just stood, sky-watching, perhaps, and others wrote and scratched, making their marks.

"But it's all forgotten," I said.

"Doesnae matter. The folk who did them will know."

It seemed so sad. "There's other things to do. Things that really matter."

Del's eyes met mine for a moment, then she looked away. "People think you're nothing," she said fiercely. "They give you a grotty flat and the benefit each week, and that's you – end of story. Well, to hell wi' that. If it gets up their noses that I'm writing on the wall, great. I'm no' bothered about years ahead, it's just doing something now."

"But you can do things, Del – you're terrific!"

"Who're you kiddin'."

"But you *are*!" I was too upset to worry about finding words, they were all there. "You know such a lot that I don't. I've been feeling awful this whole week because you'll think I'm totally wet, but I couldn't look after a wee sister and cope with everything the way you do."

"Yes, you could," Del said flatly. "If you had to, you would."

"I wouldn't, I'm sure I wouldn't."

"You look after Barney."

"Not on my own."

"If your mum and dad went off somewhere for the day, you could, okay?"

"I suppose so."

"Well, it's like that. You just do it for the day. Every day. You shouldnae put yourself down – you're all right."

She'd done it again. We were talking about me instead of her, and I'd completely lost the thread of what I was trying to say. I frowned ferociously, trying to get it back. But before I'd sorted it out, Del said, "Talking of Barney – where is he?"

In that whole moor, there was no sign of him.

Fifteen

Del was already scrambling up the heathery slope to where she could get a better view. I was only a few paces behind her, but for someone with a battered knee, she was moving amazingly fast. "There he is." she said.

He'd wandered away to where a narrow stream runs through boggy grass, with a couple of half-rotten planks across, and was floundering about, almost knee-deep in peaty mud. What's more, he seemed to be heading for an even deeper bit.

"Barney!" I yelled, "You'll get stuck! Come back!"

He turned and shouted something, but turning back made him lose his balance, and he pitched forward onto his face. He grabbed at a tussock of grass and managed to haul himself up, but the whole front of him was covered in mud.

My feet were getting wet as we went down the hill

to the boggy bit, and I bent down and slipped my sandals off. Del was behind me by now, but I saw her stoop down as well, and said, "Not you! Mum would kill me. Here, hold these." I'd seen what Barney was after. There was a sheep a little ahead of him, deeply bogged and unable to move for the weight of her sodden fleece. Her lamb was standing nearby, bleating piteously, and the ewe answered with a throaty rattle. Her eyes were staring, and her head was back as if she was exhausted.

Barney, talking to her all the time, had almost reached the ewe.

"Hang on!" I shouted. "Wait for me!"

I squelched in beside him, and together we hauled at the sheep. She felt as solidly planted as a tree, and it was terribly difficult to get a hand-hold in her wet, greasy fleece. Barney started to moan, and I knew how he felt. I said, "Go the other side of her, Barney – let's try to get her front end up."

He worked his way round, then stooped and pushed his hands under the ewe's neck. He hauled, and the sheep bleated, but didn't move, and I had the nightmare idea that he might pull her head off.

"Try for a leg," I said. I dug my hands down past her chest, feeling my way down to her knee, then pulled it upward. Barney did the same thing, and the ewe began to move. Sensing that she had a chance of getting free, she started to struggle. Barney shifted to her hind end and heaved mightily – and in the next minute, with a gloopy sucking sound, she was out, hauling herself through the shallower mud until she reached a patch of grass. She stood there for a moment, with the lamb butting at her although he was old enough not to need milk any longer, then set off across the plank bridge and up the hill, the lamb following.

Barney and I were absolutely plastered in filth, and he had lost a welly, so I went back in and fished around for it. When I waded back with it, Del said, "What do you look like! Wish I'd a camera!"

I emptied the muck out of Barney's boot, and Del added, "That was great, though. Well done, Barney! What a hero!"

And Barney hugged her.

So that was Del, nearly as mucky as the rest of us. Barney looked a bit abashed when he saw how muddy he'd made her, and tried wiping it off with a filthy hand that made things even worse, but then he trod on a thistle and forgot about it. He sat down, inspecting his prickled foot, and I wrung out the sock that had come off in his boot.

"Mrs House-proud washes with Daz," Del said. So

I threw a lump of mud at her, and she threw one back, and somehow it turned into one of those general mud-fights and it left us filthy and gasping and ridiculously happy.

We sprawled on the heather, and the sun beat down on us, drying the mud a bit. I was wearing shorts, so it didn't matter much, but Barney's jeans were totally sodden, and you wouldn't have known they were supposed to be blue. He wasn't bothered, though. When it was time to go, he put his wet wellies on without complaint, though he drew the line at the socks. He said he'd carry them, and set off up the track dangling one from each hand, making his aeroplane noise.

We tried to sneak in round the back without being seen – but it was no good. Mum spotted us through the kitchen window and was out like a flash, and even Ross looked down from his room next door to see what was going on. He grinned and held his nose as if we stank, and Del flicked him a cheerful V sign.

"What on earth have you done now?" Mum asked.

"Sheep," Barney explained. "Boot. Sheep, and Fran and me . . ." He went into a pantomime of hauling the sheep out and losing his boot, grinning all over his face, and it really was very funny.

Mum was completely flummoxed. "Sheep got your boot?"

"Fran got my boot. Sheep . . ." And he was off again.

"Well, I don't know," said Mum. "Come on in, for heaven's sake, and let's get those filthy jeans off." She looked at Del and me, and said, "If you girls would like to use the shower first, I'll get Barney sorted out when you've finished. Oh, and Del, if you bring all your dirty clothes down, they can go in the machine and you'll have them clean to go home tomorrow."

"Thanks," said Del. "That would be great."

Dad came through from the shop and looked at us, and didn't say a word, just put his hand over his eyes and slowly shook his head.

That evening, we went out to the Carrach Bar for a meal, as it was Del's last night. Barney was still on about the sheep. He'd developed it into quite a performance, and the way he falls about laughing when he gets into one of his pantomimes, you can't help laughing as well, though there was a party of tourists at the next table who clearly thought we were raving.

After all that mucking about on the beach, I was starving hungry, and Del must have been as well, because both of us had wolfed down our lasagne and chips long before Mum and Dad had finished. But of course, Mum was trying to get Barney to eat as well as talk, and that always takes a bit of time. It didn't matter – we were in no hurry. We finished off with those Italian chocolatey puddings whose name I can never remember, then coffee, and the whole thing was great.

There was still a glow of daylight in the sky as we walked home, and the shape of the hill was clear and sharp. Although it was about ten o'clock, you could see the grass and stones, and that the sheep sheltering by the day-warmed rocks were chewing rapidly with their eyes shut. I'm glad I don't eat grass – having to munch everything twice must be horrible.

Del was very quiet, but it didn't matter – the silence seemed comfortable. We walked on for a bit, then she said, "It'll be different at your new school." And I knew I'd decided.

"I'm not going to the new school," I said.

"I thought you wouldnae. Have you told your mum?"

"Not yet."

"She'll be upset."

"I know. I feel awful."

"Aye, but she was saying people shouldnae do things because of what their parents want. Remember – in the hospital?"

I couldn't make that excuse. "It wasn't just what Mum and Dad wanted. They only suggested it because I was miserable at Broray High."

"So you think it's all right now?"

"Don't know about all right. Better, though." I was going swimming with the gang on Tuesday. And there was all this – the clear sky, the narrow road winding along by the sea. Crazy to think of leaving it. "I must have been mad," I said.

Del seemed to understand. "Maybe you were. How would you know? I mean, there's times I think my dad's off his head, but he thinks he's the only one with any brains. And there was an old guy used to hang round the school, a total nutter – he'd feathers and sweetie wrappers and the like, pinned all over his coat. We used to dare each other to go and give him a crisp packet or something." She paused, remembering. "He didnae like crisp packets, he'd get in a real fury. He wanted wee shiny things, bright coloured. Those pink wrappers off Raspberry Ruffles were his favourite. If you gave him one of those, he'd smooth it out really carefully, and go shuffling off with it. But you could see he thought he was seriously okay."

"Scary."

"Och, there was no harm in him. He wouldnae hurt you."

"No, I mean not knowing." Barney didn't know, and that was a blessing, because he could be happy – but I'd always thought I was normal. The lucky one, the okay one. Perhaps you couldn't expect to be okay all the time. Perhaps it didn't matter.

Del grabbed my arm suddenly and said, "Hey, look!" Out on the rocks, a family of seals had arrived in that mysterious way they have. A few more were in the sea, and they all had their heads up, watching us.

"Oh, magic," said Del.

Barney had seen them as well, and was burbling excitedly, all for scrambling out there to try and get closer.

"Not just now, Barney," Mum said. "The tide's up, look, there's too much water. "You can look at them tomorrow, when you can walk over the sand."

They might have gone tomorrow – you never know with seals. But Barney didn't know that, and he didn't know, either, that Del would be gone, too. He was going to hate that. And so was I.

When we got home, Del went off upstairs to pack, and I sat gloomily in front of the television with the others. I hate football, but Dad and Barney like it. I don't know why I sat there, really – something to do with giving Del a bit of privacy. Something to do with not wanting to see what she packed. There was still this unspoken thing about the Talky Bear and I was in full flight from all that. Better to forget it. Write it off as something that would never be explained.

But Del had other ideas. When I went upstairs, she was sitting up in bed, waiting for me. And frowning.

"Fran," she said, "will you do me a favour?"

"Sure. What is it?" But I knew.

She held out the Talky Bear. It was powder-blue with its remote control tied round its neck in a blister pack. "Give this to the woman in the shop. Please. I'd do it myself, only it'll be too early tomorrow when we go for the boat, she won't be open. Tell her I'm sorry."

Butterflies the size of helicopters were whizzing around in my stomach. When I told Del what I would have to tell her, she'd know that we'd gone through this whole week on the assumption that she was a

141

thief, but saying nothing about it. I sat down on my bed. My face was flaming. "I'd do it for you," I said. "Honest, I would. But the thing is – Dad paid her for it."

Del stared at me. "Oh, no," she said.

I felt terrible. In our efficient family way, we'd tidied it all up and smoothed the bad feeling over. Smoothed over Del, too, as if she was just a problem that had come our way, and would depart again, dealt with. "I'm really sorry," I said.

Del scrambled out of bed and fished one-handedly in her rucksack for her purse. She sat down and tipped the contents into her lap, counting it quickly. There were coins and a five-pound note – not very much altogether. "Six twenty-three," she said. "See, I bought that stupid spray can." She scooped the money together and held it out to me. "Look, give this to your Dad. Tell him I'll send him the rest when I've got it. Or –" She picked up the Talky Bear – "he can give this back to the woman."

I shook my head. "Del, I can't do that. Don't you see? It's not that I don't want to help, but I know what Dad'll say. Why didn't you come yourself? Look, he's still downstairs. Go down now, and explain."

"Jeez," said Del. She looked terrified. "He'll kill me."

"No, he won't. I'll come with you if you like."

She gave her head a distracted shake, but still didn't move. "I cannae," she said.

"Go on. He'll be all right, honest. Just explain it was something you really wanted—"

Del gasped. "Fran! It wasnae for *me*! It was for Sylvie. She's always wanted one – all the wee kids in her school have got them." I started to apologise, but she went rushing on. "See, Dad says we're no' to have pets, and I can see it, I mean, we're four floors up, and Sylvie was that upset, me coming on holiday without her, I wanted to get her something nice. She loves animals. And I had this ten pounds pocket money. Only I bought some crisps and stuff on the boat, before I got sick, so some of it had gone. So I didnae have enough."

"Go and tell Dad," I insisted. "Tell him all that. Go on."

She gave me a desperate stare, then got to her feet, clutching her purse and the powder-blue toy. "Well, I know what *my* dad would say," she said. And she went out of the door like a prisoner going to execution.

Waiting for her to come back was terrible. I crossed my fingers and prayed that Dad wouldn't let me down. If he gave her a big telling-off after all my promises, I'd absolutely die. I could so easily imagine Del coming silently back through the door, white-faced and bitter, getting into bed without a word.

It seemed a very long time. Then I heard the sitting room door open, and Del's voice saying, "Goodnight – and thanks!" She came running up the stairs, and was beaming when she came through the door. She was holding a sheet of flowered wrapping paper and a card, as well as the purse and the Talky Bear.

"He was really nice!" she said. "I told him I'd pay the money back, but he says there's a bit left from what the Holiday Scheme gave him for my keep – so we're going halves. And Sylvie will get her pressie. Isn't that great?"

"Oh, *good*." I was as relieved as she was.

"He went on a bit about stealing," Del admitted, and her face turned a little pink. "It's right enough. People who run wee shops cannae cope if they get the stuff pinched all the time. I've never been into it really – not like some of them. There's kids at our school do it all the time." She beamed again. "And your mum gave me this wrapping paper and a card for Sylvie. Look!"

The card was from our shop, one of the ones with a puppy holding a slipper. I'd seen them on the rack under the Blank Inside section so often that I never thought of anyone actually liking them.

"She'll love it," said Del. "You got any Sellotape?"

So I went off to get her some.

Sixteen

And now it's Saturday afternoon, and she's gone. I'm sitting here on my bed, and the room seems very quiet and very empty. Del's bed has been stripped, and the duvet and pillows are stacked on the end of it in a tidy white pile. The sheets are out on the line on the sloping green behind the kitchen. Mum only uses the tumbler for emergencies like Del's things yesterday. Things smell fresher if they've been out in the sun, she says, plus it doesn't use any electricity.

I'm trying to write to Del like I promised. I dug out the paper Gran gave me yonks ago, before she died. It's got rabbits on the corner. I've written my address, and found out the date from the calendar in the kitchen and put that on as well. Letters are so difficult.

* * *

Dear Del,
You only went home this morning, but I
promised I'd write.

Why can't I think what to say? The whole week is churning about in my head, from the dreadful start of it right up to this morning, but I can't put it into words. I just wish it could go on happening.

This morning was miserable – at least, the start of it was. Del had gone all quiet, like she was when she first came. She'd put on her black tights and gelled her hair into spikes, though it was darkish brown now instead of beetroot, and when Mum asked her what she wanted for breakfast, she just shook her head. Mum went on about how Del would be hungry by lunchtime, and Dad pointed out that the crossing would be quite smooth today, no need to worry about being sick on the boat. Barney made his concerned noises and passed the marmalade and sugar and cornflakes and everything else he could think of, but it was no good. Del was pale and silent, and she drank half a cup of tea, then left the rest.

I was no help – you can't cheer anyone up when you're feeling terrible yourself, and I kept thinking what a shame it was that the week had to end now, just as we'd got things sorted out and were getting to know each other.

Mum was being determinedly cheerful. She jollied us into the car, Del and Barney and me in the back, and Dad driving, and off we went over the hill, for the last time. The early morning was still fresh and cool, but there were no clouds in the sky, and you could see it was going to be a scorcher later. Barney had been grumbling a bit because he wanted to go and see the seals. We'd promised he could see them later, but he wasn't happy, and the general atmosphere on the back seat was distinctly heavy.

Things improved a bit when Mum pointed out some deer, away on the horizon where you could hardly see them. Barney cheered up at once, and started telling some rambling story about how we'd been to a film show in the village hall and had to stop for a group of stags that were standing about on the road. Dad chipped in, explaining to Del in over-the-shoulder snatches how the deer come down from the hill in the winter, and make a nuisance of themselves, rooting about in people's dustbins and spreading rubbish all over the place.

"Go on?" Del said. She turned to look out of the rear window and said she wished she had a camera.

Maybe I'll send her a picture of a stag with this letter, if I ever get it finished. There was a good one on the kitchen calendar for February, and we've finished with that, so I could cut the picture out for her.

The boat was coming in as we drove along the shore road in Garvick. Her black-and-red funnels looked very bright in the morning sun, and a wisp of dark smoke started up as the steering engines came on to bring her round into the berth. There was hardly a ripple on the sea, but the tranquillity only added to my gloom. Why couldn't we have had a storm today, instead of last week? If it had been really rough, the boat might not have run, and Del could have stayed a bit longer.

No use wishing. Dad parked the car, and we all got out. The gangplank was hoisted into place, and people started to come off. Among the first was the dreaded cardboard woman, Mrs Mountford. The Duncans and Kerry McGuire were up there to meet her, waving and smiling. Incredible to think I'd wished we were having Kerry instead of Del. You could see she was totally thick. Then, of course, we were waved at as well, so we had to go over and join them.

There was a lot of fuss over Del's wrist. Mum

gave Mrs Mountford a note from the hospital, and explained that Del would need an appointment at a hospital in Glasgow, and Mrs Mountford tucked the envelope into her handbag and said, "Right." Then she gave Del and me one of those glances that mean the adults want a private conversation, so we went off and leaned on the railing of the Pier.

Fish were swimming down there, dark shapes idling in the shadow. We watched them for a bit, then Del said, "All right, being a fish." She was wearing her big earrings again this morning, and a lot of mascara.

"Boring," I said.

"Not if you're a fish. You wouldnae know any different."

The boat's cafeteria crew were lugging black binbags of rubbish down the gangplank to dump in the skip. Gulls flapped and screamed. The minutes were slipping away.

"I hope you'll come again," I said. It sounded so stupid, like the things landladies say to departing guests, whether they mean it or not.

"Be great," said Del. But she didn't smile, and I could tell she thought it wouldn't happen. Maybe the Scheme was only for one holiday, no repeats.

Desperately, I tried again. "Mum and I go to Glasgow sometimes, if we need something like shoes. Maybe we could see you there."

"You'll no' be comin' to Castlemilk," said Del.

"Isn't it near the centre?"

"No."

Then Dad came over and said, "Time to be off, Del. Mrs Mountford and Kerry are going aboard."

Del nodded, and picked up her Mickey Mouse rucksack.

"All right, Della?" said Mrs Mountford. "Got everything?"

"Aye."

Barney suddenly clocked that she was going, and burst into a loud wail. He flung his arms round Del and hugged her tightly. It was one of our full-blown scenes, everyone talking and persuading, and Barney bawling and hanging onto Del, and even when Mum at last managed to detach him, he went on grumbling and sobbing, and wouldn't take anyone's hand, just shrugged away

"Well, I can see you've been popular, Della," Mrs Mountford said brightly. "Are you going to say thank you for a wonderful time?"

Stupid Kerry thought this meant her as well, so

she beamed again and said "It's been really great, thanks."

Mrs Duncan said, "You're most welcome, dear." Her husband glanced at his watch. You could see they'd already been thanked to death and wanted to get home and put their feet up.

Mrs Mountford went on looking at Del expectantly, and Del tried to say something – and burst into tears. "I don't want to go!" she wailed like a little kid. Mum hugged her, and Barney flung his arms round both of them, and Dad put his hand over his eyes and said, "Here we go again." People going up the gangplank cast startled glances at us, and the Duncans looked embarrassed.

"Listen, Del," Mum said as Del mopped at her eyes with a mascara-blackened bit of tissue, "this isn't the end, my dear. You can come again, you know. Never mind the Scheme, you can come and stay with us lots of times. Can't she, Jim?"

She looked at Dad, and just for a moment, I held my breath but he said as easily as anything, " 'Course you can. And bring your wee sister."

"Could I really?"

"No problem."

I was in tears as well – I'm hopeless when things get emotional – and Del hugged me in turn. "Listen, thanks for everything," she said. "Like – the wee crabs and all that."

"It was you who found them. I'll write to you, promise."

"Me, too. My spelling's terrible."

"So's mine."

We were both in tears again – and suddenly Mrs Mountford started to laugh. I didn't know she could. "Well, if that's not a successful holiday, I don't know what is!" she said. And I heard her add quietly to Dad, "If you do it again, we'll meet the expenses, don't worry about that."

"Great," said Dad.

The crewman at the top of the gangplank shouted, "Hurry along there, please!" – so that was it.

We stood there while the ropes were cast off and the boat started to move away. The Duncans were still waiting dutifully, and all of us waved. Del and Kerry and Mrs Mountford had gone up to the open deck, and waved back until the ferry turned away in the broad circle that headed her towards the mainland, then they were hidden from sight. Nothing was left but the white curve of the wake, spreading across the sea.

So here I am, trying to write this letter.

Stare out of the window, nibble the pen. The sea's all sparkly out there, like it was when we found the hermit crabs. What can I say?

I miss you.

ALL THAT GLITTERS

Pippa Goodhart

A gripping fantasy – based on a true-life story ...

Twelve-year-old Locket Morrain can have anything she wants – except her freedom. When her wealthy mother dies, Locket finds herself living with a father she barely knows and is surrounded constantly by bodyguards and the high stone wall that rings her father's estate.

Desperate to escape. Locket hatches a magical plan to make gold enough for everyone ...

Only then will Locket finally be free.

ORDER FORM

0 340 73679 8   ALL THAT GLITTERS   £3.99 ☐

All Hodder Children's books are available at your local bookshop, or can be ordered direct from the publisher. Just tick the titles you would like and complete the details below. Prices and availability are subject to change without prior notice.

Please enclose a cheque or postal order made payable to *Bookpoint Ltd*, and send to: Hodder Children's Books, 39 Milton Park, Abingdon, OXON OX14 4TD, UK.
Email Address: orders@bookpoint.co.uk

If you would prefer to pay by credit card, our call centre team would be delighted to take your order by telephone. Our direct line *01235 400414* (lines open 9.00 am–6.00 pm Monday to Saturday, 24 hour message answering service). Alternatively you can send a fax on *01235 400454*.

TITLE		FIRST NAME		SURNAME	

ADDRESS	

DAYTIME TEL:		POST CODE	

If you would prefer to pay by credit card, please complete:
Please debit my Visa/Access/Diner's Card/American Express (delete as applicable) card no:

Signature .... Expiry Date ....

If you would NOT like to receive further information on our products please tick the box.   ☐